A Surfeit of Mandrake

Edited by

Chaz Wood

A Surfeit of Mandrake,

Being an Anthology of Works
by
Diverse Dundonians

Edited by Chaz Wood

For

Fenriswulf Books

"The Tragicall Historie of Kit Marlowe", " 'Maranatha': Overture",
"Liebesrasen", "Berlin Girls", "Young Legionnaires", "Northern Eyes",
"In Memoriam", "Old Frog", "Wolf-Age"
© Chaz Wood

"The Devil You Know", "A Crime Uncommon", "Cerulean Blue",
"Fragmentation: King John to prince Arthur of Brittany", "Mouse",
"Plaster Saint", "Too Goth to Live, Too Drunk to Die",
"The Toebone of St. Giles", "The Edinburgh Lawyer"
& "The Train"
© Lesley-Anne Brewster

"The Labourer's Hire" and "Novice"
© J.I. Stuart

"Fragments of a Time to Come", "Personal Evolution", "Return to Dun-Shi",
"Witch's Knowe", "Modern Myths", "The Sennachie"
© Frang McHardy

"Godz Almighty", "Leper Messiah" & "Clan Clash"
© Chaz Wood & Frang McHardy

"Mandrake" Cover artwork by Frang McHardy

The following is a work of fiction, and any similarity to real persons, events or institutions is purely coincidental.

First published by Fenriswulf Books, 2008.

1st. Impression

ISBN 978-0-9559891-0-0

Fenriswulf Books
C/o Dubton Farm Flat
Brechin
Angus
Scotland
DD9 6RA

info@fenriswulf-books.co.uk
www.fenriswulf-books.co.uk

About the Contributors

Lesley-Anne Brewster – Writer

Lesley-Anne Brewster is a writer, a Mediaeval re-enacter, and a practising witch. She started writing as a child, winning a Cadbury's chocolate poetry competition at the age of eight. She still likes writing, and she still loves chocolate. Her motto is, '*If you're not happy with it, change it; and if you can't change it, change the way you look at it.*'

Frang McHardy – Illustrator, Writer

The lesser-spotted Frang's natural habitat is the drawing board, which he has to return to frequently. Here he can be spotted idly daydreaming about naughty nymphs and wayward witches. If you're really lucky, you might get to see him scrawling some far-fetched fable he has spent aeons concocting. Years of retreat inside his own warped mind have resulted in the kinds of deranged visual excretia reproduced here. His diet consists of ancient history, otherworldly music, pulp picture parables and the odd sobering shot of reality (just for kicks).

He is now an endangered species, due to the extinction of a multitude of species of publishers, and the declining interest in visual storytelling. The Frang may have to evolve rapidly to adapt and survive in the harsh realm in which he currently resides.

J. I. Stuart - Writer

J. I. Stuart started writing Science Fiction in his early teens, and at the ages of 17 and 18 succeeded in winning, on two successive occasions, the magazine short story competition run by his school – a very large senior secondary in Glasgow. His next publication, 35 years later, was a treatise on Victorian glassware that has sold nearly 50 copies! In the interim he has produced several full-length Sci-Fi novels around the *'Enigmatic Klylii'*, which he hopes to be in a position to publish quite soon.

Mr. S. is a retired BT manager who lives in Broughty Ferry with his wife and their two Labradors.

Chaz Wood – Editor, Writer, Illustrator

In summer 2008, Chaz set up Fenriswulf Books, originally as a means to market his self-published series of novels. 'Maranatha' was his first published full-length work of prose. Bitten by the self-publishing bug, he immediately recruited others into the do-it-yourself drive, and 'A Surfeit of Mandrake' is the result. In his spare time he watches movies, studies history and mythology, draws comics, bounces around to loud music and plays bass guitar in Jeremiah, his Dundee-based rock group.

Editor's Note

Here I stick my oar in before allowing the reader to wander among the gathered offerings within. Feel free to skip this, browse at will and examine at your leisure, for the 'thing' with anthologies is that an editor can try too hard to please everyone. In collecting this material, there was no plan. I simply asked talented people I knew for some of their 'stuff', and that was that. As a result, we get certain recurring themes, either by some cosmic synchronicity, or by pure chance. We have Christopher Marlowe, in the form of a broad cod-Elizabethan farce, and later in a subtler tale of friendship. We have witches, warlocks, and strange powers at work. We have fragments and memories of Scotland and her past, mythical as well as actual, and we have flights of pure fantasy, science fiction epics and down-to-earth fragments of reality. We end with a revised depiction of the ancient Norse myth of the Fenris Wolf and his misbegotten family, he who inspired this entire publishing exercise in the first place and whose visage and name will adorn the covers of all future ventures.

Why a *Surfeit of Mandrake*? It has a dark, olde-worlde, even medieval ring to it, suggesting an over-indulgence in some half-remembered folk remedy. Because it seemed to fit with the overall tone of what I was seeing, and compiling. It even went so far as to completely inspire the short story which features it, a tangential postscript to an unfinished comic strip. Yet, it seemed to gel, and form some kind of stream-of-consciousness arc between worlds and minds. Synchronocity.

So here you have it, a diverse collection indeed yet bound by common themes. Dundee-based writers and artists, yet compositions that take us far further afield – to worlds unknown out there, or deep within us. I do hope you find something within that pleases you. If you do, or even if you do not, let me know in any case. We all thrive on feedback and comment.

Thanks due to everyone who contributed, and who showed enthusiasm for this project from the beginning, including the staff at Dundee's Borders. This wouldn't exist without you.

And go easy on the Mandrake.

Chaz Wood
Brechin,
Samhain 2008

Contents

	Page
The Toebone of St. Giles: - Lesley-Anne Brewster	11
Berlin Girls: - Chaz Wood	14
In Memoriam: - Chaz Wood	16
The Train: - Lesley-Anne Brewster	17
Young Legionnaires: - Chaz Wood	18
Northern Eyes: - Chaz Wood	20
Overture to 'Maranatha': - Chaz Wood	21
Leper Messiah: - Chaz Wood & Frang McHardy	25
Plaster Saint: - Lesley-Anne Brewster	40
Liebesrasen: - Chaz Wood	44
The Devil You Know: - Lesley-Anne Brewster	47
Clan Clash: - Chaz Wood & Frang McHardy	51
The Tragicall Historie of Kit Marlowe: - Chaz Wood	57
Witch's Knowe: - Frang McHardy	72
The Edinburgh Lawyer: - Lesley-Anne Brewster	73
The Sennachie: The Keek Stane: - Frang McHardy	83
A Crime Uncommon: - Lesley-Anne Brewster	89
Return to Dun Shi: - Frang McHardy	96
Fragmentation: King John to Prince Arthur of Brittany: - Lesley-Anne Brewster	101
Old Frog: - Chaz Wood	102
Modern Myths: - Frang McHardy	106
Cerulean Blue: - Lesley-Anne Brewster	107
Mouse: - Lesley-Anne Brewster	111
The Labourer's Hire: - J.I. Stuart	115
Fragments of a Time to Come: - Frang McHardy	141
Novice: - J.I. Stuart	149
Too Goth to Live, Too Drunk to Die: - Lesley-Anne Brewster	179
Godz Almighty: - Chaz Wood & Frang McHardy	182
Wolf-Age:- Chaz Wood	193

THE TOEBONE OF ST GILES

By Lesley-Anne Brewster

1 The Wife's Tale

He was not long for this world. Alys knew the signs, the subtle scent of fear controlled. As though his sunken eyes already saw their way to Purgatory, and he had not words were fit to speak of it.

He was a decent man; and she - who had been traded to a tyrant, and then danced off by a merry rogue who on his death bed howled his whore's name – valued decency, and comfort. Feared now for her own, for three dead husbands, each enriching her, were meat enough for taint of poison.

So, all though she did not love him - all her heart belonging still to Hugues, who had wound her round his lying tongue, yet woken something in her which her merchant, in his decency, could never satisfy - she had resolved to seek the intervention of a saint on his behalf. Buy him a miracle.

The pardoner was young. One of that new breed who roamed Europe, now as scholars, now as mendicants, and, curiously, he made her think of Hugues. The way his brows arched... something feline in his smile...some vague thing...

It was pleasure to converse with him. To play, round talk of prayers and sealed indulgences, the ancient game of baiting then denying. Take delight in being a woman of abundant flesh.

He had been keeping something covered as he rooted in his satchel. Only showed it when she, teasing, pressed him to. Inside a lidded casket, on a bed of scarlet taffeta, he had the keeping of a toe bone of Saint Giles. But it was not for sale. Or so he thought.

She had been obliged to offer more than she had intended. Still, she had won it. Now she clasped it to her bosom like a line thrown to a drowning mariner, and went smiling to her husband. Soon he would be well.

Soon he, and all things, would be well.

2. The Pardoner's Tale

The merchant's heifer had been flirting with him; which was unexpected. He had heard rumour of her husband's mortal canker from a trading rival. Sought the village out; and having taken care to have in his possession such a relic as would prove entirely efficacious, were it genuine, lingered piously about the sorry-looking chapel nearest hand the merchant's house.

Sold fourteen copies of a benison of his own composition; coming close to throwing the rig by being spectacularly drunk the night before and failing to consider that a bone is, to a straying hound, no more or less than that.

Perhaps the saints were looking out for him.

But her...he had played it cautiously at first. Uncertain whether, in his precious state, he had been construing her aright. There was her spouse - her third, i' faith, - weak-knocking at Death's door, and there was she, as hungersome for compliments as comfits. It was inconceivable.

He had shown his wares, reserving best for last. The toe bone of Saint Giles; ostensibly entrusted to his care by Cardinal Ruffio in Rome.

What, sell it ? Such a treasure was past price. Yet in the keeping of a lady so devout, and given the extremity of need...et cetera, et cetera. He had talked a month to reach a fortnight's end. Wrung less from her than he had thought her good for, finally settling out of thirst, and fear that she might add her doughty virtue to the scale.

He stood and watched her as she plodded off. What pity for the merchant. He had heard the fellow had more coin than wit, but to have bought on such a silly, uncooked dumpling of a woman, who, if that performance gave her measure, was already looking out for his replacement...

Well, Hell mend him as it might.

3. The Toe's Tale.

Saint Giles lived in the seventh century, in the empire of the Franks. A hermit in the wild wood which at that time bearded thickly round the broad mouth of the Rhone, his sole companion was a tame albino doe who fed him milk. Until...

One dawn a famous king, King Charlemagne (or Childibert, or Flavius) shot the white-haired holy man by accident whilst hunting deer. A king who subsequently went so much in peril for his soul that he sought evidence in confirmation of the hermit's sanctity, securing him canonisation and founding a monastery in his name; which monastery gradually became a famous pilgrim site. With healing power so strong that the fatally ill could be cured by the simple donning of his coat, Saint Giles became the patron saint of cripples, beggars, hermits, horses, spur-makers, lunatics and nursing mothers; winning a day (September 1st) in the Salisbury calendar of saints.

Depicted in iconoclastic art pierced by an arrow, with his tame doe by his side, his intervention was invoked against cancer, sterility in women, sudden madness, lameness and ' the terrors of the night '.

He also - if the contents of the reliquaries of medieval Christendom were to be credited - had forty-seven toes, sixteen of which were animal in nature.

Hugues De Vere, who had been the second husband of Dame Alys Merchant ; and was buried to the east side of the chapel of Our Lady of the Sorrows, five miles distant of the village where his former wife now lived, had not been blessed with such a plenitude. Had been possessed of merely ten toes; of the which, in consequence of John the Pardoner's nocturnal search for a relic small enough to fit inside his ring box, only nine remained to rise with him upon the Day of judgment.

Berlin Girls

Chaz Wood

I fell in love with a Berlin girl just the other day
Saw her in the chorus line of the Domino cabaret.
From 'midst the same old regulars, incognito on the town,
The boys (who might be girls), and the thugs in black and brown.

I've seen the Horror, Lust and Ecstasy on stage at the White Mouse,
The Behrenstrasse's Babel, Berlin's wildest house;
There's love and pain aplenty, dressed in shiny leather boots
But chains and whips and naked hips are nothing when you see
With your own eyes
This fantasy.

Throw me another cigarette, I've got something to say
Fell in love with a Berlin girl, oh just the other day.
The rakes and drug-filled nationalists can tell me what they like,
But we all know that anything goes, and everything's alright.

In this midnight, starlit world there is something for everyone
A thousand ways to be disgraced, to stretch your sense of fun;
In black and red they'll strut their stuff until your are sore,
But if, like me, you fall for one, expect no sympathy
Or loving eyes, just -
Reality.

In Memoriam

Chaz Wood

The music's on, but nobody's home
There's a storm of change blowing through the town.
Still stroll these empty streets alone,
As the Sunday sun comes rolling down.

I see them gathered in the park
Stop outside the gates and have a smoke.
The clouds overhead are dark
And I think they all just missed the joke.

So kinks and queens and deviants, come take your seats
Popes and priests and martyrs, tenants of Cato Street
Droogs and dregs and hooligans, let's not forget our sons
Out fighting for their country, for footballs, not with guns.

When did you last see your father? Was it many years ago?
Did he finish up a casualty, in Falklands' mud and snow?
Schoolboys, take a lesson – start it at page one
Bleeding hearts need surgery, now see how it's done…

And there's a breathless hush in the close tonight
The playing fields glow with a holy light
The church clock stopped at a quiarter to nine,
End of the innings – end of the line.

England's day-dreaming, when will she wake up?
Another storm in a royal wedding teacup?
So tell me a story, tell me a lie,
Some tale of glory and a reason to die.

The Train

Lesley-Anne Brewster

This is how it happened.
I was there; and Colin, he was there ; and
someone else, although I can't remember
whether it was James
or his twin brother, Joseph. Anyhow, the train…
No. I should start a little further…
We were playing ' Bonanza '. By the railway siding.
By the fence made out of standing sleepers. Like a cowboy fort.
And when the noise came
– solid, screaming metal, arcing rainbow sparks –
we were what actors call 'in character'
so Colin (he was Hoss) said :
' Wanna mosey down an take a look-see ?'
So we moseyed.
Wish we hadn't.
There were bodies. No. Not bodies. Bits of people
And whole people staggering round and round
In rags and blood and some of them just standing.
Standing. Staring..
We were staring, too.
Three wee boys, staring. At
The train.

Young Legionnaires

Chaz Wood

Remember in the days when we were young
Back in '78, when music used to be fun?
They said, 'Form your own band now, you know three chords'
And like a thousand others, I took him at his word.

We had a bleached-out beach boy with a broken guitar,
Said he once met the Pistols in an East End bar.
We had the flash and the Clash and the devil may care,
And we called ourselves the 'Young Legionnaires'.

Robespierre, Danton, ou sont mes heros?
Come out to play now, we need ya on the dance floor.
King Mob's waiting, he's got nothing to lose,
Except his powdered wig and his blue suede shoes.

Put the blame on the Dame, boys – those days are gone.
Thought you were a bishop? You were only a pawn.
But hist'ry met the future on the gold-paved streets,
In the dawning of something that was more than a beat.

Northern Eyes

By Chaz Wood

Every winter has a tale, somewhere in the nights unfolding
Every tale a hero – or some forgotten moral
When you got no place to go, feel the cold and come inside now
Hey Coldly, let me feel something I can warm my hands on
This Arctic Night.

Somewhere in a windy dugout, soldiers sit in passive trance
Passing cigarettes around
Somewhere in an open swing park, Old Grey sleeps upon the bench
Dreaming that he'll live to see the dawn

Now let me show you, things you only ever get to see
Through Northern Eyes
Come let me bring you things you never had back in Osaka
With Northern Eyes.

Every winter's night, see the dance of snow around you
So hard to see when the night comes down to drown you
Don't you give up now, Summer soon is on its way
Wish you could hibernate? Wake up when it is all over,
This Arctic year

Back in a frozen dugout, soldiers sleep in fitful breaks
Dreaming hopes of peace and home
Now in an open graveyard, Old Grey rests eternally
Peacefully at home, and warm at last

Twelve centuries ago, Viking ravens flew the pagan sky
Pecked Northern eyes;
Shores of ice still shimmer now, bitter frontiers without love or life
These Northern eyes…have seen so much.

OVERTURE to *Maranatha*

By Chaz Wood

The streets of Zvornik lay broken, the black outlines of buildings stark against a grubby smudge of sky. The bombs, the shooting and the screams had all subsided to the silence of the grave. Only the dead remained to see this pale grey morning and all 100,000 acres of the abandoned place.

The silence was broken by a regular rhythm; steel ringing against stone, the still scene given movement by a tall figure striding. His dress was black, from beret to boots. Leather gloves slid an expensive foreign cigarette from a breast pocket filled with trophies and lit it with an American lighter as Captain Gavrilo Silajdzic snaked his way through the remains of the old City of the Bell Tower. The smoke of undying fires merged with mist which crept in from the River Drina and veiled the tops of the tallest buildings which huddled together like homeless children. The beauty of the mountains and the river valley was blackened, all nature banished. He saw no evidence of any historic towers now as he turned a corner, nor would he have cared if he had, for ahead of him lay his final destination, the end of his six-day journey from Sarajevo.

The Church of St. George stood at the end of the road, its half-open doors revealing blackness beyond, but still the most welcoming sight he had seen that past week. As he entered, he brought shafts of cold daylight with him to stimulate sounds of life inside, the first he had heard all day. He saw patches of blotchy skin shuddering beneath tattered shawls and blankets, mumbling sorrow. *Peasants.* Unpleasant, pestilent.

Crouched in front of the altar was a tattered vestige of a human being, balding, grey-bearded, muttering prayers into the scabrous remains of his hands.

"Milan?" Silajdzic asked. And again, louder.

The priest looked up to the figure which cast its shadow upon him. "Who's asking?"

Silajdzic stepped aside into a pool of light and drew in the air a five-pointed star with his left hand. Milan found his feet and hugged the other man like a brother. "Oh, you've come. Thank God. A terrible time we've had of it but somehow, the Church still stands. I see it as a sign from God. It's the only reason I'm still here."

"For divine protection?" Silajdzic surmised with a laugh.

"Yes, exactly." Flustered with excitement now, Milan began rummaging through bags and bundles beside the altar. "I have it here." He produced an old leather holdall and removed a gathering of rags from within, about two feet long and bound up with string. "Men died getting this out of Montenegro. Take it to our people, help them bring victory and peace in God's name." Silajdzic took the gift and began to pull away the rags, but Milan's knotted fingers intruded. "No. Don't show it. Just get it out of here, to our brothers, as fast as you can."

Silajdzic spared the other man a defiant glance as he continued to pull the object into general view. "Just a brief confirmation. Is that permitted?"

The priest was outraged. "You think I'd deceive you? We're all in this together, aren't we?"

"This *is* a war, Father. Besides, Father Rattus said no-one can be trusted."

Milan's voice hardened. "Well, I don't trust that English Rat either. He has knowledge he won't share, and feeds us scraps like the hobo's dog whenever he sees fit."

"He is a man of God, I understand. Like yourself." He finished uncovering the prize and held it up. It was a strange item; a metal spearhead over twenty inches long, enveloped in sheaths of gold and bound with wire, and a vertical slot which held an iron nail.

Satisfied, Silajdzic bound it back up and slid it into his backpack. "Thank you. Hope that losing possession of this doesn't bring disaster upon your Church." The thought carved Milan's face with furrows of concern. "Don't worry, Father. I promise you, the Holy Spear will be in good hands."

As he went to leave, Silajdzic heard a sharp breath pierce the air behind him.

"Your uniform...you're SDG. Who - why are you - working for *them*?"

Silajdzic turned, a deep snarl pulling his face into angular chiaroscuro.

"In times of war, one must make hard decisions. If you don't like the idea of that, Brother – *Father* - then you shouldn't be here."

"And I don't like the idea of Zeljko Arkan holding that spear, and his fascists seizing victory."

"*Mors stupebit et natura, cum resurget creatura*, Father. These are dark days for us all. And Commander Arkan doesn't hold the spear, I do. Anything else you want to add, or are you finished trashing my leader and my comrades?"

Fear drained the colour from Milan's complexion. Silajdzic's quotation from the Dies Irae had struck a discord within him, the Latin hymn describing the Day of Judgment which seemed now so dreadfully appropriate. There was no denying that death had struck, and all nature was shaken.

"Tell me – truthfully, Brother – that you are faithful to us. Tell me I am doing the right thing here."

"I know what is right, for I know what my people have suffered over the last thousand years. Slaughtered by Turks as they fought for their freedom. Massacred and burned at Montsegur, raped and enslaved by Stefan Nemanja."

"They were heretics – Cathars, Bogomils –"

"They were my *ancestors*. And now you, who I do not see leading anyone, or raising a gun in defence, tell me that I am wrong to fight for *my* country, my beliefs, and to avenge all that blood spilt by Papal decrees and Muslim scimitars?"

"I didn't say you were wrong." Milan argued.

"Five hundred years ago, we could have ruled Bulgaria without any Roman clerics vomiting lies from their pulpits. For they would have been on their knees, crying to their God and to Satanial." Spots of spittle, trailing his words of fury, landed across the priest's forehead. "All *your* kind."

"What are you saying?" Milan choked on his despair, his realisation wringing glistening grief onto his cheeks.

"I'm saying, the Black Sun is rising, Father. But you're not going to live to see him, and nor are your holy brothers going to stop him."

The unseen 9mm semiautomatic spat five rounds through the priest's chest, throat, and stomach, five wounds which formed the points of a five-pointed star, a pentagram or pentangle. Silajdzic thought it an amusing gesture, branding the corpse with the symbol of its own order. His satisfaction was disrupted by cries and groans from the pews.

"What are you doing!" the woman howled, a lacerated soprano rising to the rafters. "Stop it, stop the killing!"

For a second Silajdzic contemplated putting her down where she stood. Then he saw her child, a boy of no more than ten or eleven, follow fearfully in her footsteps.

"Please, don't hurt my boy. Don't hurt him," she begged as her fears washed out her anger. "Do what you will with me, but leave him alone."

He saw her gaze wander downwards, where Milan's blood flowed in five rivers toward the altar. He drew down the headscarf which covered her matted yellow hair, ran his fingers through long wispy strands of soot and dust. She hadn't lived long but hard, and the toils told on her skin and in her eyes, red-rimmed and weeping. The gold crucifix around her neck made him smile; so much for the power of the Lord. He tested her reaction, grabbing her heavy breasts through her shirt, and she closed her eyes in tired resignation. She had suffered this before, and was numb to it now, a deep-throated groan of surrender her only acknowledgement of his frantic actions as he pulled up her dress and bent her over the back of the nearest seat.

The boy stood confused, wondering what the pair of them were doing. He was very afraid of the man in the black uniform and had no wish to anger him. He looked a lot like the men who had shot his father and watched him die screaming, eaten alive by wolves.

A minute later Silajdzic stepped back, wiped her blood off himself using the hem of her skirt and adjusted his clothing.

"Please, leave us be now." Her voice held the reedy undertone of agony barely restrained. She had taught herself not to scream, not to cry, and to save her breath to thank God for continued life.

"I'm not going to touch your son." Silajdzic assured her. "Rather, I want him to grow up knowing how useless his God was at this moment, and force him to ask; where was my saviour, my Christ, when I needed Him? Where was my God? And one day, I hope, he shall learn the truth."

She raised her head from the shadows to look upon her son again, to steal a grain of love from the hand of pain for one moment. The child had advanced nearer, happy to have heard his mother's voice again when something wet and warm slapped him across the face and neck. He wiped at it with his hands while Silajdzic walked past him to the door, sheathing his hunting knife as he went. Just before he stepped into the dusty white chamber of daylight, he turned back to look at the boy, a muddy Breugel orphan beside the corpse of his mother, whose slashed and ruptured throat spewed crimson puddles around his feet. Silajdzic tossed the woman's bloody crucifix onto the floor and laughed aloud, the sounds breaking the peace of the tomb.

"Suffer little children, and forbid them not to come unto me: for of such is the kingdom of heaven, eh, *Father*?"

Illustrations by Frang McHardy
Prose by Chaz Wood

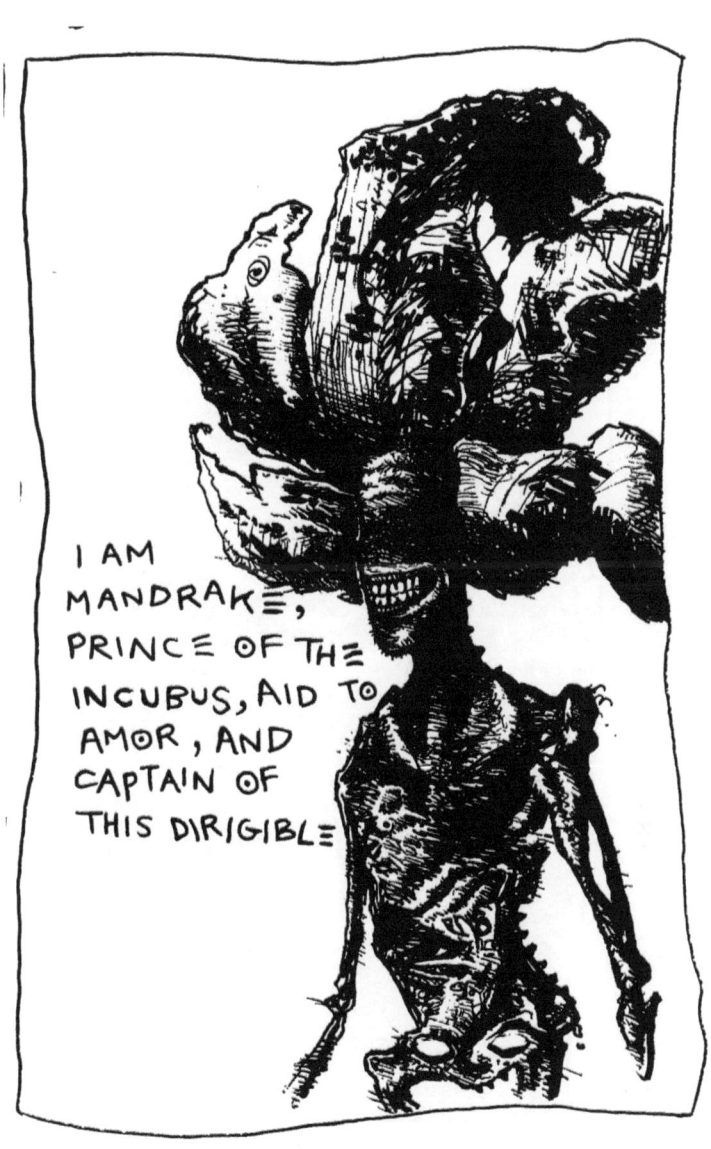

So, that's how it began.

    The highland spring had uncoiled in my mind, driving me through the landscape in which we had landed. No matter where I looked, the shark fin of Mandrake's dirigible cut a black segment out of the sky, and my sight. If this was a world and its mythology created by an eyeless root-man, and I was its saviour, then it had to be a very bizarre cosmos in which I now walked, trundled, seeking something. Reason, explanation. A way back to my flat, and the joint I had until recently been enjoying.

    I missed the sensation of the rolly-up which Mandrake had taken from me, the damp paperyness on my bottom lip. I was obviously stoned out of my box, which might at least have the benefit of making me appear divinely-inspired to impressionable passers-by, for the duration of this strange delusion.

Domes and spires welcomed me as the cityscape began to unroll. The potential converts to Mandrake's cause had been few and far between in the grassy outlands, twisting paths bringing me into contact only with an unfair few. The moons were high and bright and I was in with a decent shout. The city was where it would be at, the heart of the scene. I walked onward, a backward glance reassuring me that the fin still cut the sky, still patiently awaiting my return- no, I hadn't woken up, and I was still in hock to the pilot of the grinning shark-toothed blimp.

The blackness that had swamped me during my space-out moments, when Mandrake had first crashed through the dimension of reality into my flat, had begun to lift. I saw no point in questioning. I was what I was, a wandering messiah, driven by an unknowable demagogue of black and leafy princehood, incubus deluxe, haunter of minds and penetrator of dreams. Lassies too, if the legends I recalled were right, but that was another matter. Or was it? Aphrodisiacs took many forms. It didn't matter I was no longer sitting on the sofa in a top-floor flat in Lochee Road, listening to Gong going click-taka taka –click taka-taka on the hi-fi because I was too washed-out to get off my arse and stop the record from jumping. It had only cost a quid anyway from Groucho's, and besides the cover was cool.

Brickwork and nightmare protuberances beckoned me in. There were enough fragments of the reality that I had left behind me to convince me that I really was tripping, not literally over my feet although some of those paving stones were evidently laid by someone with no understanding of geometry. If Great Cthulhu had invented Lego, and built a city out of it, the results might have been expected to resemble what I was looking at. Eyeballs and organic bulbousness hung above me, things moved through the sky which were connected by telescopic means to towers that seemed to have been built from random mechanical and kitchen appliances, and decorated with left-overs from an abattoir. Buildings with appendages that looked grafted on, rather than built, or even designed. It wasn't a comfortable promenade, for sure, but no messiah's path was ever free from thorns.

I stopped at the door of the first likely-looking edifice, a curved and pepperpot-like structure with double doors made of brass. I was met there by someone, a man, I realised with some difficulty, having to peer beneath the layers of patchwork blanket. "Business?" he asked, in a voice that sounded strangely sampled from a Gong album. The little tugs back to the world – my world – were reassuring. If I could play along for long enough, I could probably wake up, most likely with a cracking headache. And damn, the cupboards were almost empty, so I'd have to run down the hill to the wee shop on the corner. Meantime, this was my chance to give it the messiah spiel.
"I bring the word of Mandrake, Prince of the Incubus and Aide to Amor."
"And what is the word?"
"Frank."
" 'Frank' is the word?" he sounded sceptical, shuffled blankets back. Tried to get a better look at me, revealed a crooked tooth and a half-moon eye.

"Well, not really. Frank is my name. But I'm pretty new to this messiah thing, so go easy on me."

"No messiah ever had an easy time of it, sonny. Christ was crossnailed, Mani skinflayed and John the Baptizer headchopped on the behest of a naked harlot. Don't even ask what they did to poor Polki the Seventh-Day Recidivist."

That all made perfect sense. I'd been reading a book about prophets and religions before I'd rolled that joint. The joint which Mandrake had confiscated, and which I was still obviously still suffering the effects of.

"I'm really sorry to have bothered you. I'm afraid I don't even have leaflets, or a nice illustrated gospel to leave you. Maybe I'll just walk on and find a corner in the street, and shout until someone listens."

"That'll be a good way to see the inside of a madhouse, if that's what you're after. So, messiah is it? You realise what you've taken on here?"

"I thought I might develop a feel for it. Like riding a bike, or creative writing. I hadn't really given it a lot of thought. It was rather…thrust upon me, so to speak."

"Came out of the sky, did he? Jumped on you at random – pulled you out of some alternate reality and brought you here to spread his word?"

He knew the whole story. The whole strange grainy monochrome ink-blotch story, fired by burning paper and weed. How could this strange blanket-clad character in need of cosmetic dentistry have known?

"I'm afraid to say so, yes. Would you like to join me?"

"Mandrake is not what he appears. A roving parasite, feeder of life. His roots are deep, and many. Beware whom you preach to."

"How do you know all this?"

"Look, what do you think happened to his last messiah?"

"I don't know. Not sure I want to know."

"I think you should be on your way. Best not to stop at too many houses – people don't like chaps interrupting their dinners or lovemaking with religious downspeak. You can try the street corners if you like, but be warned. Hecklers can be cruel."

As the door closed to a stripe of light, I felt an uncommon boldness possess my foot, enough to plant it in the path of the door's arc of closure.

"Yes?"

"Sorry," I apologised. "But, what do you think would happen if I…*don't* want to be a messiah?"

The crooked tooth grew some equally crooked colleagues in the dark. "You really don't want to think about that, Frank. Go, now."

I did.

The street corner was draughty, due to a rising wind, and I was getting nowhere. I'd found a box to stand on, which made me six inches taller but didn't incite the crowds much. I let my hair blow in the wind and rolled my eyes a lot, but they weren't buying it.

"Mandrake," I boomed. "I bring the word of Mandrake. Mandrake is Prince, a King in waiting. Giver of pleasure and joy. Peace and love flow from his black and veiny fronds. Peace, love! Love…is all you…need. Love is…the greatest thing. A many splendoured thing. Like Mandrake."

I realised I was beginning to feel very stupid. People had no interest in Mandrake and his fronds. Maybe they'd heard it all before. I looked around. No sign of the sharkfin, me being well within the city's enclosure now, so I abandoned my box and crossed the brick-lined avenue to a purple pagoda that Kubla Khan may have decreed, or Coleridge imagined while poppy-piping.

A person stood there by the door, looking right at me, and by virtue of his poise I assumed him to be a doorkeeper of some kind, and he seemed to have been expecting me. I strode up.

"Business?" he asked.

"Ah, pleasure." I tried, hoping for a recess from the preaching for a while.
"Pleasure. Well, you've probably come to the right place. Come within."
He turned and led me through the door. Smoke greeted me as I hurried inside. So did noise, lots of it, and the smells of the kinds of pleasure usually associated with a good pub – from the days before they stopped us from smoking in such establishments and condemned us all to shiver on krebbies like little knots of smouldering lepers.

I moved through the heaving glut of flesh, excusing myself as I went so as not to offend anyone or spill an expensive drink (or even a cheap one, being without coinage of any kind, as is usual when the dole cheque's late). Faces leered and peered, samples of conversation snatched at my ears then dispersed again.

Made myself comfortable in a tall stool seated with yellow velvet at what resembled a drinks bar. Eye-pleasing females congregrated at the other end, laughing and waving thin hands in the air. I was approached from the other side of the bar and asked my preference by a thin, angular man in denim overalls.

"Peace and love," I sighed. "The word of Mandrake."
"I have beer. Also wine, for the ostentatious, and brandy for the bold. Choose."
"Beer."

A pint glass was served, warm and bitter, though no payment requested. Free drink, and the freedom to smoke (although I had left my baccy tin and other accoutrements back in Chez Frank) - whatever next? I tasted froth and left a white moustache of foam on my face, which brought much merriment to the gaggle of girl-geese at the other end. I smiled, wiped up, drank deep. Being a hopeless messiah was surprisingly thirsty work.

I was half-way through the pint when one of the gigglers was beside me. She was not old but had a mature glow behind her eyes, dark and deep. She wafted plaid and jingling bracelets as she sat side-saddle on the next stool.

"Are you a preacher?"
"Not really. If I am, I'm probably going to be out of a job soon."
"We saw you outside earlier. Booming about the Prince of Amor and stuff."
"Thanks," not knowing really why I was grateful. That someone in this wild daydream was independent enough to speak to me, perhaps.
"I like amor. And black, veiny fronds." She poked a finger toward my glass. "Goes well with beer."

She pulled from beneath her plaid wrap a little blackened thing, which, after she'd stopped waving it under my nose, looked exactly like a miniature version of the Dirigible's Captain himself. She winked and nodded urgently toward the door we had entered.

So that's how I ended up back at her place, a small circular enclosure that rather resembled the inside of an egg. Ovoid and womb-like, quite appropriate considering our activities in and out of her bed, and she screaming "Yes, *yes, Mandrake!*" over and over and over throughout as lassies are wont to, lashing and grinding in what looked like a religious ecstasy and felt like forever.

Perhaps this was the way forward for this reluctant messiah, I wondered, as she snored beside me and I took another sip of my liberated beer (being a hopeless messiah was very thirsty work). It certainly beat being crossnailed or skinflayed or headchopped (though so far, the naked harlot had been most exhilarating) or whatever happened to Pokey the whatever the hell he was (though I suspect my blanket-wearer made that one up on a whim).

I looked at what was left of her little root. The torso alone, the limbs and head having already been torn asunder and ground into spicy, thick drinks for us both. The sharkfinned dirigible captain had not been wrong – he, or his finger-sized kin, were indeed a great aid to Amor. In fact I'd never had Amor like it. I could get to like this very much indeed, as much as any drug. I wondered vaguely if this was what the youth of this Lego Cthulhu city considered 'cool' – the underhand aphrodisiac which filled their spare time and brought such pleasure and togetherness. I would be the supplier, the dealer, the distributor of the masses' opium.

And as I lay and stretched beneath the curved curiousness of the ceiling, the future became clear, as clear and bright as that eggshell around me. I would bring Mandrake to the people, in root form. They would partake of his body, his flesh, and in the ensuing ecstasies, they would be one with Him, the Prince and the lord of the Incubi. He would bring joy and pleasure and Amor to all, and all would worship him, and I would preach of his greatness and face eager flocks, all desiring to consume their god, their master, and enjoy the joys He brought them.

As a messiah, of course, I would have to partake of His holy self as well, no doubt with a great number of favoured disciples. This was looking good. I didn't know if it was what the eyeless one had in mind, but without any instruction or much in the way of a heads-up, not even a walking to Damascus knees in the dirt and eyes awash with light etc. kind of epiphany – it was the best I could come up with at short notice.

So that would be that then. I folded my arms under my head and drifted off to sleep on board a big wide grin. I didn't really mind which world I woke up in – mine or hers (er, what was her name?).

Woke up cold. Shivering. I grabbed at her plaid but it wouldn't budge. She wouldn't budge either so I pulled harder. Then the plaid came free, and a thin pale hand flopped onto my chest. I was about to knock it aside when I realised the hand was cold and just a little stiff.

Not looking good. I looked at her. Eyes closed, trickles of dried-up something at mouth's corners. I shook her. No life. Checked her pulse. Nothing.

Definitely not good. I got dressed, clothes and boots going on the usual places without any thought. What did I do? Run back to Mandrake? Seek a policeman? Pinch myself (though that never worked)?

Get the hell out quick. Run like a bastard, run and see what happens. Hell, it's only a dream. Drug-induced keech of the highest order (only hope I remember half of it when I awake, so I can write it all down and call it literature).

Meantime, needs must. Door opened alright, led me back out onto the street. Walls and alleyways all around, a Cretan labyrinth, me such a
cretin and Mandrake the minotaur lurking somewhere within or without. Would he be happy, or vengeful? Let's run like a bastard and find out. Could always plead diminished responsibility (wasn't me, Guv – self-administered). Or insanity, inanity more like, though the unspoken fate of Polki the Seventh-Day Thingy troubled me somewhat.

What did your last messiah die of? It sounded like a bad joke. I was running. Running like a bastard. What could I do? She was dead, I had responsibilities, at least until I straightened out. Keep on running, meantime. Messiah and leper now, probably an outcast, though not my fault. But since when was that any excuse?

Another alleyway opened up. Graffitti every bloody where. This world just as susceptible to ad hoc art and sloganeering as mine. Serpents, devils, squiggles, obscenities all squirmed across the walls. As did the name of the Prince of Incubi, writ large in hadal black. A bowler-hatted droog, knife-thrusting, leered out at me from a mural. At any other time I would have stopped in admiration. Now, I only stopped in terror.

Mandrake stood before me, filling the alley, head-fronds waving in the wind. His shadow fell upon me, and his skinless mouth bared hideous teeth. The huge black gladius in his hand told me he was displeased.

"I'm sorry." I screamed, throwing myself upon his mercy, and the pavement. "I didn't know what to do. It wasn't my fault. I didn't mean to fail you."

The sword-tip screeched across the badly-laid alley floor. Drew a line in font of me in the stone.

"Frank, Frank. What am I to do with you?" the voice chiding, holding bitter resonances. "Do you know what happened to my last messiah?"

Headshook, vigorously. No, no idea. Wanted to know, though.

"Died."

Ah, now wasn't that a surprise. This was not proving to be a good trip. I wondered if I should sell my entire stash after this and become a reformed junkie. Move out of Lochee Road to a nice place in Carsnoutie, perhaps. No, really. I was all done with this dope shite after this one.

The sword tap-tapped. The other hand did things with his lower abdomen, unhinging what had looked like body but seemed now to be armour. Codpiece fell aside on gooey strapping, a giant stem – stalk unleashed before me, pulsing with ill-concealed passion. The root of Amor, alright.

"The cause? *A surfeit of Mandrake.*"

And that's how it ended.

Plaster Saint

By Lesley-Anne Brewster

I can't talk about it.
You said to write it down. That it might help.
I tried before, but a lot of the pictures have blanks like holes burned into cellophane. Most of the sounds are noise.

I remember the dressing-table backed against the window. Plaster statues of the Holy Virgin and Saint Patrick staring at my Mai's pink nylon bedspread; at the knitted poodle dog that held her nightie, and at Mai. Who had lovely lipstick lips, hair black as chip pan smoke, and five of us to different daddos.
　'Sure, they've seen some holy sights " my uncle Pate said.
We'd a lot of uncles. Brylcreemed men with yellow fingers and a bob to spare for sweeties. To begin with. Some had cars. Mai'd charm them into driving to the seaside or a posh hotel where we got crisps and lukewarm ginger. Some were too fond of The Drink, or else would think to lift their hands. But Mai was up to them. She was a battler.
　Uncle Pate was different. He was Mai's real brother.

On the nights she decided to stay in, we all did The Twist with Chubby Checker. Sang like John, Paul, George and Ringo. Shared pie suppers from the Fry Bite.
　Pate would carry in the bath, and Mai would wash the five of us with Avon soap on facecloths, always starting with the cleanest. Tell us stories of when her and Pate were living in the country, picking strawberries and raspberries and tickling fishies. We would fall asleep, all five, to the flickering blue light of the black and white telly; the lonely trumpet sound of Coronation Street.

I remember the loveliness of it, of being a part of a shifting knot of arms and legs beneath the Barras blankets, breathing in a faint tart whiff of pee and ash from off the fold-down sofa. Dreaming Enid Blyton dreams.
　Then Pate, who was seventeen when I was nine, would seem like one of us. Like Joe or Lenny, only bigger; and so handsome, with his thick black wavy hair, his big brown eyes and big white teeth. And I could love him then. I did.

But there were other nights. Nights Mai went out in sling-backs and a cloud of
Elnette hairspray; never mind who cried. And Pate was left to baby sit.
Nights when he'd whisper :
　　'Rosie...'
Lift me in my vest and nightie through to Mai's room. To the big pink bed, the knitted poodle and the Holy Virgin and the plaster saint.

You're supposed to remember your first time. I don't.

He'd been doing it forever. Not to me. Not really me. I wasn't really there. Not all of me. I never really felt him doing it. Not any more. But when the wetness came, when I could smell the stink of it and had the power of him and he said:

'Promise you'll no' tell.'
I always promised.
Who could I have told?

My teachers? They were nuns; the brides of Christ. The virgin brides. They had spied me for a hell-bound sinner even without my telling; and my big class were as bad, saying dirty things about my Mai, and putting chalk and spittles on my blazer.

I would always get them back. I knew the worst of them, the bullies, hid
their own wee dirty secrets. Put collection coppers up their knicker legs; or had a daddo at Barlinnie, or a granny took the gas. And I could battle. I enjoyed it. When they had a hold your hair, and fists and feet and knees and all were coming at you, you could seta about and roar.

I didn't have the words or heart to tell my Mai.
She awful loved her brother.

'Him being such a bonny bairn was why the Grays adopted us from out the Home' she would tell us. ' He just stood up in the office and he told them – he was only eight, as well – that it was both us they'd to take, or he'd not go.'

'Mai, are we bonny bairns enough to get adopted?' I had wondered. Just in case the polis used detectives to find out about folk's uncles.

Mai put both hands to her mouth. As if she was trying not to laugh. But later on, when she told Pate, she gret and told it like a holy story.

I was thirteen when it happened. Seeing Mai all puffy-faced and snarling from being skint again and getting low on fags, Pate dug through all his pockets. Found twelve bob.

' G'on to the dancing' he had urged. 'I'll mind the bairns.'
I wasn't old enough.

I lay along the very outside of the couch, heart battering like a sparrow at a stair head window. Watched him drink six cans of Tennants lager; watched him watch a Hammer horror film: The Twins of Evil, it was called.

Pate liked his horror films. He had sat there smoking as he watched it in the dark. Sat smiling; drinking. Flicking at the filter of his cigarette and fiddling with the open razor he had bought after a Wednesday night run-in with the Tong. Sat waiting for the squealing and the squirming to go quiet; the smothered farts and snottery snoring to begin. Then he whispered :

'Maggie...'
I was too old.

So had I been protecting my wee sister, like they said? All I remember is the plaster saint. The pearly handle of the razor, and how smooth and warm it was. Remember staring up at Mai; and all the blood, but nothing more.

And writing it all down, it doesn't help at all.

The Devil You Know

By Lesley-Anne Brewster

General consensus in the Ballendreich cafe-cum-shop-cum-Post Office was that they were well rid of John McGillivray. That lad had been a sore temptation. Quite the worst the toun had seen since Tor Mackay, who met a wasteful sorry end away in Aberdeen.

With John, like Tor, they'd seen it coming, mind. Right from the day his mother sailed in asking after aubergines, whatever a body might want with the like of they. No wedding ring. Both legs bare naked as a tinker's, that for all she came from money. You could see it in the bairn's clothes, if not hers.

'I'm Kate McGillivray ' she'd said. Without being asked. 'and this is Johnny.'
He'd corrected her; and him not half the size of threepence.

'John ', he had peeped, 'I'm John.'

So John he was. And at the start, there she'd be, crying round for menthol
cigarettes and fancy coffee after driving him the road to wee school in a brand new Subaru. Then bringing him, and him with both arms elbow-deep in everything, by for a poke of sweeties and a comic at the back of three o'clock, before going home to Hinder Greenie.

Hinder Greenie, where Pat Bain had raised eight decent sons; that as a farmer and a widower. She had bought it with cash money, so she had; while folk who had their own folk living round here were fair strapped to find the rental on a static caravan.

Apparently - the woman gave her past out like a Baptist parish paper - Miz McGillivray had been a journalist. In Edinburgh, if you like. She had won some manner of a prize, and thought she'd chance her arm at books.

None of your Mills & Boon, True Crimes or such, mind. No. Expository prose, it was; whatever that might be. It had no art of bearing on the bringing up of bairns, that much was sure. You would have thought his wee backend was crystal glass, the way she pandered to him.

Might well have looked for him to suffer at the school for sakes of being so cosseted, but not him. He had a way about him with the other bairns. Dancing them into deeper mischiefs than they likely would have dreamed up on their lone. Tormenting beasts and setting fires and thefts and vandalising; and then after he had a car bought by his mother for himself, it was the speeding and the window-dirling music; and the drink.

Not that they bought that up the shop; nor cigarettes, for Morag MacIntyre was well wise to the proper ages of them all. But Mr English up at the Hotel, he was as soft as new-made tablet when it came to John MacGillivray, for he'd worked up a kind of notion to the mother. Made a fine fool of himself about her, too; and all for less than John could win from any of his daft young foreign chambermaids and waitresses with just a wee bit whisper and a wink. They said he had three natural bairns, and him not twenty yet ; and that his cold indifference had been the death of more

He was a bonny devil, John, yet. With his wavy hair and white teeth and the big green eyes his easy grinning never seemed to put a spark to, quite.
He could be near polite enough when he was after something. While no doubt as many lasses were no better than they might have been, what with the Pill and all.

This latest one was different, yet: a lovely lass, wee Lucy, a wee angel. Come from someplace in Australia; else New Zealand, Mr English said. What she, like folk that come from there do, cried 'Down Under.'

John MacGillivray had watched her like a ferret at a dove. He would be there, but never with her. Aye at foremost of his friends and posturing fairly, else stood just a slant away. And while you saw disaster in it, still you had to give it down they made a handsome pair...

Sunlight chased shadows on the braes of Ballendreich, and in the small wind breathing down the summer grass, there was a scent of summer dying, cooling green. John sighed; drawing Lucy closer into him.

'You'll leave me soon.'
'John, don't. I can't…'
He wasn't listening. Such skin she had, all smooth and golden; tasting warm and salt as sunlight-melted butter. He would win, no matter what the wager's worth might cost in lies.

'Here, you could stay..' he said, as though the thought were freshly laid, 'If we got married, say. '
'Us, married ? John, I..'
'Don't you want to marry me? Am I a fling, just; just a holiday romance? I see. So that's the way of it. ' He turned his face away, although his hands stayed occupying the territory he had won to. Knowing this always worked. ' Here's my own self, fit to bursting with the love of you, and willing to do anything ; to give you anything ; and there's you, holding back for sake some lad you left at home..'
'It's not that. It's not that at all…. John? '
'Aye? '
'Did you say 'anything '? That you would give me anything? If we..you know…'
'I did.'
'Your heart? '
'It's yours.'
'Your soul? Your very soul? Think carefully, John McGillivray…'
'I.. what? ' he shrugged. 'Aye. I suppose.'
'Done.' Lucy smiled and wrapped her perfect smoothly golden limbs around him. Round and round him, cool and surging strong and strangely patterned rough; and drew him down and into her. Where all was solid, beating dark.

Well, Kate MacGillivray went back to Edinburgh. After kicking up all manner of stramash ; and never mind the bonny lass was missing with him. Fainted in the street, had Miz Mc Gillivray. Beside the Hydro. Had been carried in the shop to get a sit down and a wee bit sip of water. Tap, not bottled.

    Yet, for all the kindness shown her, she had raged. Had not been loath to cry the whole toun down ; and most of all the women of the congregation. A cold coven, she had called them. So they were. For they had seen it coming, mind.

Clan Clash

Words & Story by Frang McHardy

Illustrations by Chaz Wood

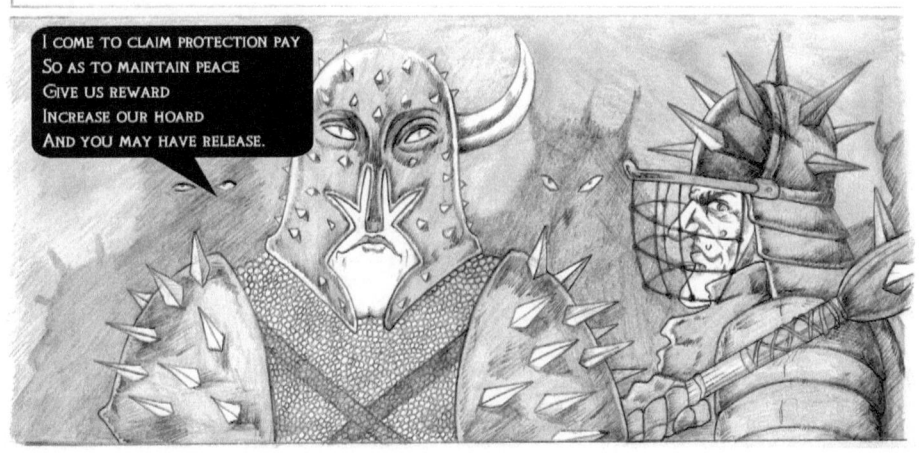

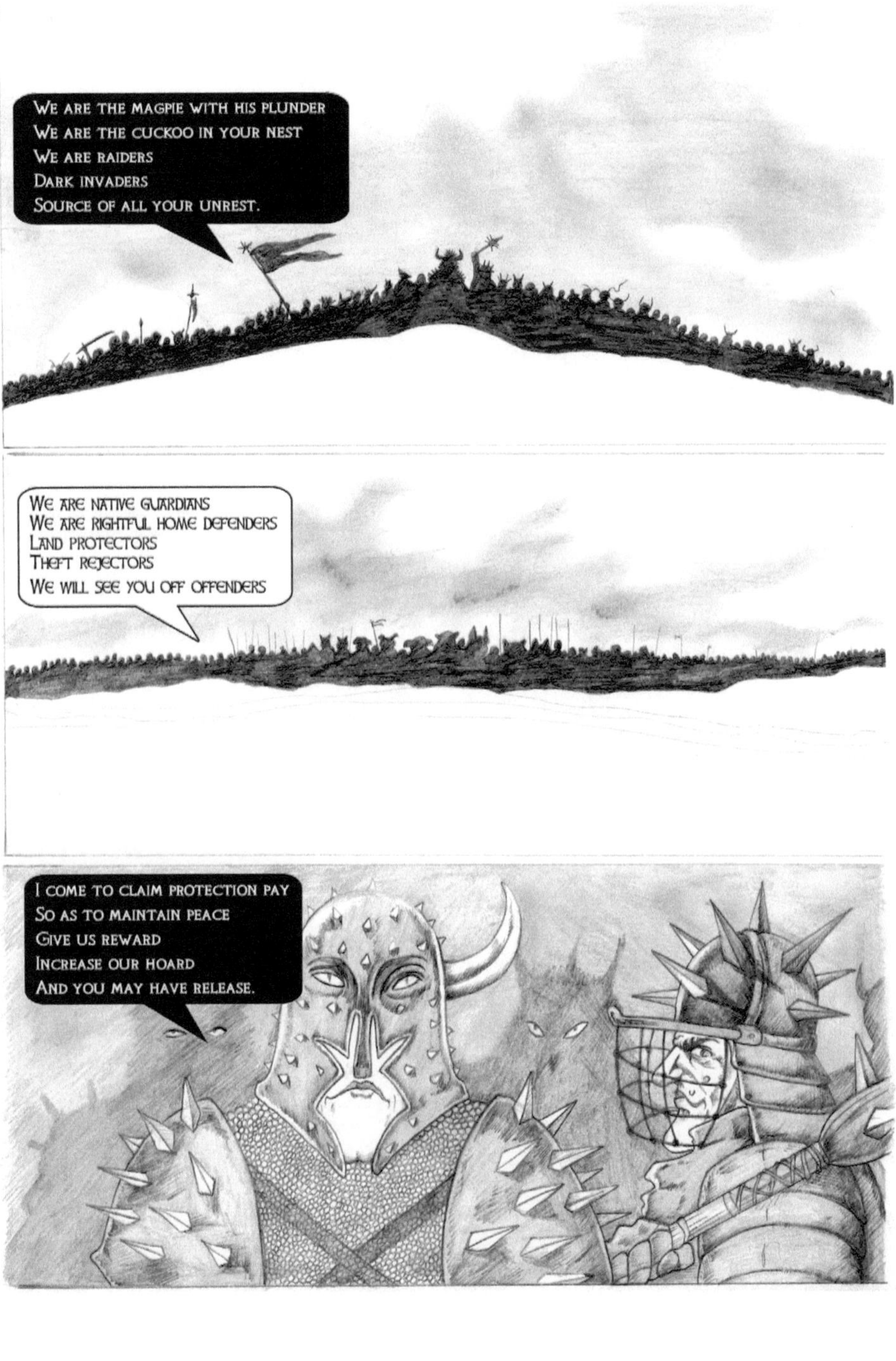

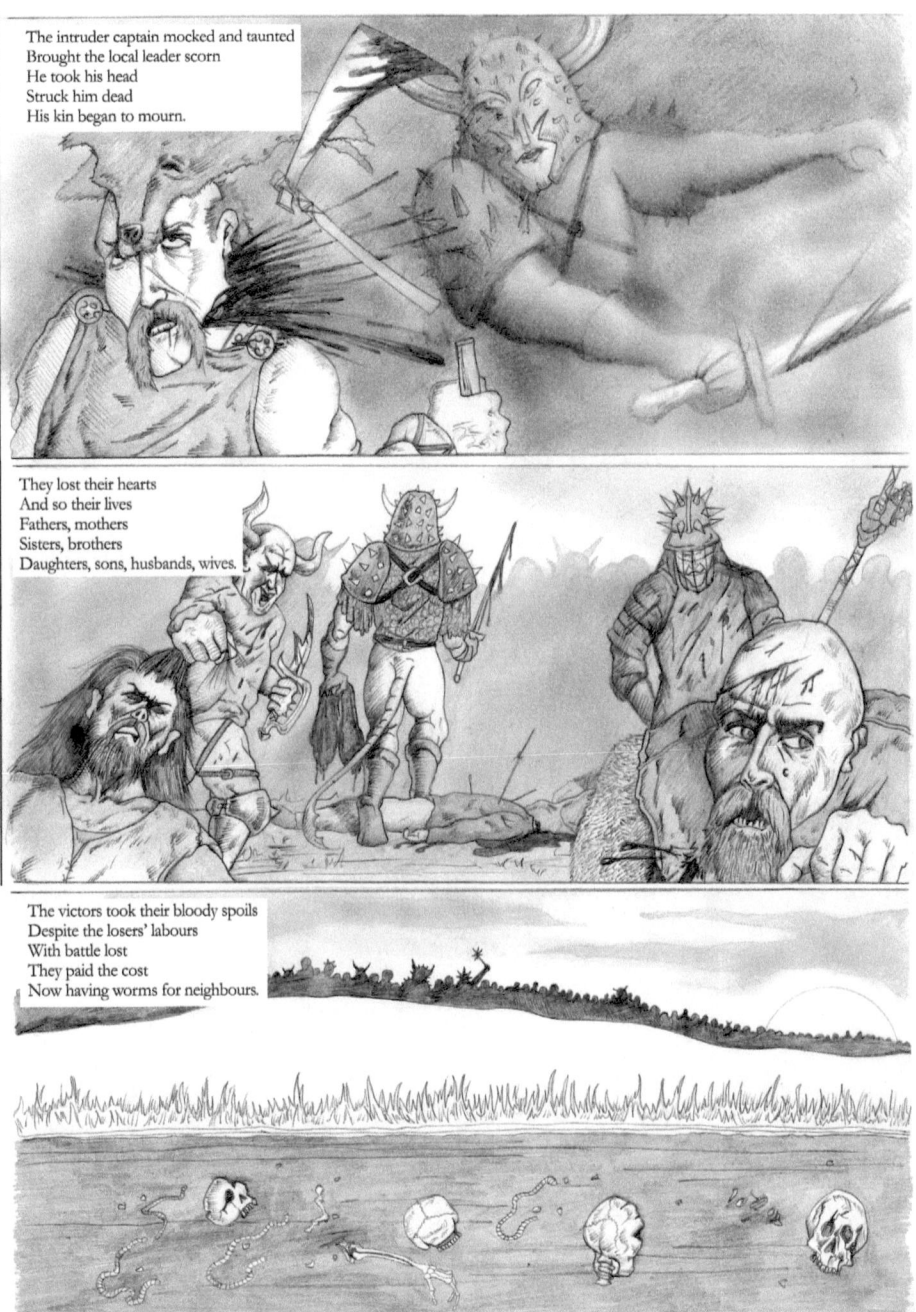

The
Tragicall Historie
of
Kit Marlowe

By C. Wood

INT: PUB. Night.
SUBTITLE: DEPTFORD, MAY 30th, 1598

A busy, bawdy pub packed with gay men, prostitutes, rent boys. Some wear sailor's costumes, some leathers, others in army gear. The women wear little more than underwear, likewise the boys. These are the actors who will perform, via various changes of scenery and costume, what is to come. This pub is their theatre, the setting for what is to follow. Enter Roger, a spike-haired punk in ripped jeans, braces and t-shirt.

    ROGER
  (In hunch-back pose)
Smelly, jelly underbelly-
Welcome to this jolly play.
Legs are limp and eyes are skelly,
Teeth are black and flesh is grey.
CD players and evenin' telly
Ain't enough for us today;
May we voice our elegy
To our late muse who's passed away
No Auden, Byron, Keats or Shelley
But one Kit Marlowe...died this day.

    OTHERS
  (Raising their glasses)
That's our kid.
  (Singing in drunken chorus)
Died this day, died this day,
Shuffled off, this merry May.

    ROGER
Bless 'is Faustus, Edward, Jew.

    OTHERS
Bless 'em all, th'unholy few.

    ROGER
  (Straightens up and blows his nose)
Enough rhyming for now...I fear my scraps of poet's wit were scavenged from the floor whence Master Marley chucked 'em. Our guv'nor, he was. No-one gave us lot better lines to read than him. We could pack 'em in every night when doin' one of his shows, every bleedin' night. Lord

>   Strange's Men are we...and damn proud of it too.

He twangs on his braces.

>   VOICE AT THE BACK
>   Strange, bloody queer more like it.
>
>   ROGER
>   By way of tribute we present OUR Kit. None of these bloody government
>   lies or tabloid exposes, mind you. The real flesh and blood man we all
>   knew and loved. He liked flesh, and blood too, but then he was human, like
>   all of us. It's what sets us apart from the angels. And now, rejoice in a
>   celebration of the master wit that sustained we mere mortals for so long.

Hasty scene-change as the cast depart for their costume changes and with the erection of a painted backdrop at the back of the pub, the scene becomes a drawing room in a gentleman's residence. Incidental lute or guitar music is played throughout by a lone sailor who hangs out at the back of the bar. Roger holds up a large card: 'The Tragicall Historie of Kit Marlowe: Writ by C. Wood, gent.' Exit Roger. Enter Walt, a distinguished-looking man in his early forties with van Dyke beard and three-piece suit, holding a screenplay. He smokes a pipe.

>   WALT
>   Young Marlove is a marvel. Lucifer himself could not bring so
>   much light to the theatre, nor wild flame such passion.

Enter Marlowe with a crash, a long-haired, wide-eyed figure.

>   MARLOWE
>   Who speaketh that name? Raleigh, what devilry
>   Ensueth here?- in thy house, by Christ;
>   And from thine own mouth? I,
>   Lucifer to some, but above God to others!

In the background, enter a demon doing a fire-eating routine, attended by Helen of Troy and the magician Faustus. These three conduct their own silent mime of the final scenes of 'Dr Faustus' as dry ice rises all around.

>   RALEIGH
>   Ah, dear Marlow. 'Faustus' is read.

He indicates the screenplay.

> The thoughts and sense of my modest mind
> All but paralyz'd by its enchantment;
> Compr'hension to all but rapture hamstrung
> By thy godly words—

> MARLOWE
> Speak not of gods to me.

Walks to the bar and draws himself a pint.

> Art thou pleased then with it?

> WALT
> Pleased; as wrapt as any man could be
> In arms of heav'nly glory.
> But I also speak of darker things;
> Things only friends like I may raise.

Faustus and Helen kiss. The demon grabs Faustus and hauls him, kicking, offscreen. Marlowe applauds them as they go.

> MARLOWE
> (yawmng)
> Raise it then, Sir Walt.

> WALT
> This secret trade, these hidden deals.
> I fear your love of Queen and Country goes too far.
> These men who hold you to their ways
> Of politics and schemes...! fear for thee.
> Too young, too brash, a perfect scapegoat.
> Walsingham's a snake, a jackal too.

> MARLOWE
> (Hasn't been listening)
> Thanks are due to thee, Sir Raleigh.
> Oft I hear the critic Greene
> Chew upon me in his squalid columns.

Picks up and throws aside a tabloid, 'Variety'-style magazine.

> Bring Faustus, and we three shall drink tonight
> To money, lust and blasphemy.

Enter rent boys to prop up the bar. Several start rolling joints and pass them around.

              WALT
            (worried)
Kit, no beer tonight; I have an audience for thee.
Some men of rank have appointed ye-

            MARLOWE
Balls to that. Sod them all.
I've better things to do than crawl
To 'gents' and 'sirs' of bastard blood...
I'll kick their pants into the mud.

            WALTER
Please!

            MARLOWE
To hell begone with pleasure, Sir.

Downs his ale and eyes Walter suspiciously.

What do you want, Sir Walter, eh? What brought you here, so late of hour?

Marlowe seizes Walt's head and plants a kiss full on his lips. Walt pulls himself away, shocked.

            WALTER
Jesus!

            MARLOWE
            (Laughs)
Yes, my son? Be this what brought you here-

Tries to kiss him again but Walt pulls back.

            WALTER
I will not have this!

            MARLOWE
Others do... many, many, ten a penny,

>   WALT
> O what wit! Breathed straight from Satan.
> May I please hear more of it.
>   (Aside, to audience:)
> Baccy, boys and beer. Volatile fuel for the shepherd poet. The
> lad's excesses try my patience. But for that, I taught him well.
>
>   MARLOWE
>   (smacks Walt around the head.)
>
> Okay, Walter, take yourself
> A flying jump or take a shit.
> Get the hint? I'm on the job.
> Now kindly run along and split.

Walt shrugs sadly. One of the patrons enters, coughing his guts up. He chases Walt as he leaves and begs a cigarette off him.

>   RENTBOY
>   (to MARLOWE)
>   Got the time, Mister?

Marlowe looks suddenly pensive. Death, robed and carrying a scythe, enters and flits behind the bar, peering down at him, unseen.

>   MARLOWE
>   Plenty. But not tonight.

The boys gradually disperse and exit until Kit is alone, leaving him to ponder at the bar with only Death for company. During Marlowe's monologue, Death pours himself a large rum and gazes sadly at the posters which celebrate Marlowe's past successes.

>   MARLOWE
> How quiet this night; what manner of fate
> Doth this chill silent breath portend?
> O, fly hence, ghost of misery;
> Lonesome spirit, infest me not!
> How eager grows the flesh come nightfall;
> How warm becomes the spirit, aflame
> With fruits of foreign fancy.
> O, love! One paltry plea I make to thee;
> Let me in thy holy chamber dwell
> That I may die for want of love,

For strange am I to Plato's passion
Have been; aye, and ever will.
I thought-I hoped-I prayed- but once
That I might love not flesh but soul-
But dam'd am I, to death, and cursed
To lewdness, lust, eternally.
Come, passionate shepherd; return to me!
Sweet boy of nature as I once was;
One honest man 'midst hordes of Huns
And Goths of ancient barb'rous mind;
Oh come, return, come, heal me now
Of bloated flesh and corp'lent soul
Aglut with lust and treacherous plans;
This world of gyps and common knaves
And plots and wiles of twisted minds.
O, thy pleasures do me move,
Return me to my May-mom bed
Of posies, wool and ivy-buds
From whence I thoughtlessly did stray,
Away from thee and thine, to foreign schemes;
And hoary shades of hell unclean
And half-reveal'd promises of gain
Which tempted me so sorely.
Domineering is the night,
Oppressive wretch, like those who move me
In their grand designs of this and that;
But I care not. For naught am I,
A lovelost shepherd, cast forth from Eden
With my words and wits before me held,
Small comfort for my forsaking of
That I held most dear and close—
But! Night rolls on, and with it, time
O time; begone! Poor Faustus' bane.

He lies down on the bar. Death ogles him through the bottom of his rum glass.

          MARLOWE (cont'd)
Now must I sleep; alone again,
With only wit and thought for warmth
And soon to walk in Morpheus' groves
Of boundless fancy; 'ternal world
Which hath no bounds nor earthly rules
From which I must return, alas.

He yawns and stretches.

> O, to be a dream, a shade,
> A satyr in some grand man's dream
> To dance and play eternally, to pipes and drums
> Of sweetest whim.
> Come hither, sleep, torment me not
> With visions of ideal days long gone;
> For time does not procrastinate,
> Nor heaven's spheres idle on their paths;
> Thus am I damned, expel'd
> From idylls of such simple joy
> And doomed to wander, without pause
> Down this pit-filled track a fool called life.
> Enough! What's done is done.
> Done am I, and thus to sleep.

He extinguishes the lamp behind the bar. Death's head glows in the dark.

> DEATH
> So fine a bough,
> But best be cut before one wilts.

Removes from his robes a bound book with Marlowe's face on the cover. He turns to a page marked Year 29': it is blank. Automatic writing appears on the page: 'Terminat author opus.' Fade to black.

INT. Pub. Night.
The light goes up. A scenery card depicting a foul dungeon has been erected. The walls are covered in nightmarish blow-ups of the British Museum woodcut showing the massacre of the Huguenots on St.Bartholemew's Eve. Roger stands centre stage, holding a card, reading: 'Tom Kyd, known associate of Kit, undergoes torture by command of Privy Council on charges of heresy, of writing the Dutch Church Libel, &c.' Kyd is handcuffed to the wall, dressed in rags. A Hell's Angel-type jailor inflicts various tortures. Knocks.

> JAILER
> A gent to see ye, poxy louse.

Enter MARLOWE, in disguise. Exit Jailer

KYD
Who art thou, stranger, robed and quaint?
Remove thy hood, for I would see
What angel comes to me at such
A dark and dismal hour?

MARLOWE
Balls of Beelzebub! Kyd, my voice alone
Ought well to tell ye-

KYD
Marlowe! Christ
Against all hope- what brought thee here?

MARLOWE
News speeds well. I heard of thee
And thy condition.

Drops his disguise.

So, blasphemy, is it?
Treason? Plot? Or something worse?

KYD
The libel, Kit. 'Twas not I who penned it.
And were I you, I'd flee this place
Ere they pierce and brand thyself as well.

MARLOWE
Seems to me the Dutch twits
Have skins of paper. I have read this thing,
And it amused me so, but enraged me too
That such a doggerel wit should steal
The name of Scythia's conquering king
And mine own tragic Tamburlaine.
But enough of me.

(Shout)
Who shall drag thee from thy fiery cross,
What sweet Mary lick thy wounds?

He picks up a spear and jabs it in Kyd's side.

KYD
Peace! O peace prevail, I pray!

MARLOWE
Thou dost pray? Thou prayest?
To what wooden ears dost thou now beg?

KYD
What sin committed I but 'gainst my self;
Are you damned, Marlowe? Have I condemned
Ye to glum Pluto's grasp by my words?
None but I shall cast anon
This flimsy garb my soul doth wear-
Abandon'd, to the moths of Satan's wardrobe...

MARLOWE
Even in death venom slakes thy tongue.
The truth shall slither and hiss from thee,
And danm me thus eternally.
And give up on the rhyming, by the way. Leave it to the professionals.

KYD
What can I do? At torture's mercy
I may tell ofevil things;
O flee, I beg, begone this place
Ere I sentence thee to death.
But ask I must; why dost thou hate me so?
Hast thou no pity for a man in hell?

MARLOWE
(turning to go)
We all abide in hell, sweet Tom.
This wretched hall of our own making.

Raps on the wall as he leaves. As he departs, a hidden door opens and Lucifer pops his head out, looking around. He shrugs and goes back in again.

KYD
Oh, Marlowe...what wouldst thou think had I for once succumbed
to truth?

Enter Jailer, grinning and cracking his knuckles. Fade out as Kyd begins to scream.

INT. Pub: Night.
Roger sits on the bar opposite the stage, holding a card, reading: 'HQ ofSir Francis Walsingham, Spymaster-General to HM Queen Elizabeth I'. On the stage, a backdrop of an office has been erected. Walsingham sits centre stage at a desk, reading a newspaper. He is dressed in black and looks like a cross between Mephistopheles and Big Brother. Headline: 'Superpoet in Heresy Shock!' Enter Frizer, bowing, followed by Poley and Skeres. Both are large, cockney football-hooligan types, though Frizer looks slightly more civilized than his companions. A propaganda slogan fills the wall behind the desk- 'Knowledge is Never Too Dear'.

          FRIZER
   (bowing)
My Lord.

          OTHERS
Mr. Secretary.

          WALSINGHAM
Enter, men. Take seats. I've much to say.
The Queen has urgent work this day.
For I have seen the Massacre at Paris
In bloody flesh as well as mime;
And do not care to see such sights
In London streets in mine own time.
Now then, to this, our rowdy friend.

   (He slaps the newspaper)
His antics drive me round the bend.
The playmaker makes more than plays,
He'll undo everything one day.
Now answers, gents, if you so please.
Let's bring this to a speedy end.

          FRIZER
Marlowe's scene is most unholy.
What say you, sir Roly-Poley?

          POLEY
The fuzz are onto him. Seems Tom Kyd's had his share of hassle.
If they put the pins on Marlowe too he could blow everything.

          SKERES
Bugger wants out. He'll scream and shout

Unless we take precautions.
No other way; he'll have to pay for duty with a caution.

          WALSINGHAM
Exactly why he must be silenced.
Subtle threats must yield to violence.
Frizer, you're the man to do it.

          FRIZER
But what if we...? Ah, screw it.

He bows in acceptance. All four shake hands, sealing the conspiracy. Cut to:

INT. Pub. Night.
The pub as it was at the beginning. Frizer, Skeres and Poley sit drinking beer at a table. A busty barmaid, Ellie, is on duty. Enter Roger with a card, reading: 'Wednesday May 30th, 6pm: the house of Mrs. Ellie Bull. The hour of the reckoning.'

          ELLIE
I find it most exciting that the Master Marlowe is returning here.
I wonder, would he sign a beermat for me?

The others sneer as she serves their drinks. Enter Marlowe, looking subdued.

          POLEY
      (Flicks her some coinage)
That's for the beer. Now leave us to our gentle talk.

Ellie leaves. Marlowe slowly takes his seat.

          MARLOWE
      (Picking up the bill Ellie has left)
So this, then, be the price I pay?

          FRIZER
So fine of you to get the tab. Now, to business.

          MARLOWE
Tell me, how is Mr. Secretary? Still farting sulphur? Returned yet to his horny master?

He has folded the bill into a paper aeroplane and launches it at Poley. Poley jumps up, spoiling for a fight, but is pulled back down by Skeres.

FRIZER
His Lordship...ahem. Requests your
Co-operation on a sensitive matter of national security.

He fiddles with the dagger at his belt.

MARLOWE
(bored)
Piles, is it? Syph? Still bothered by the Popists? Hang 'em all, I say.
I only did it for the money. For the thrills.
And as for those 'secret dossiers'...

Skeres gives Frizer the nod. Frizer whips out a dagger, charging Marlowe.

FRIZER
This, Marlowe, be the price you pay for treason.

MARLOWE
Scythian sabres are drawn in Deptford.

POLEY
Do 'im!

Marlowe and Frizer have a brief and violent struggle on the table as Poley and Skeres pinion his arms.

SKERES
For Her Majesty...an' England.

MARLOWE
(bleeding)
Die, life! fly, soul! tongue, curse thy fill, and die!

Frizer stabs Marlowe in the head. A black curtain, reminiscent of those found around hospital beds, is pulled around the bar area. The curtain is embroidered with a threadbare Royal Crest. Enter Roger.

ROGER
Snuffed it badly, skewered stiff.
Trials or jury? Not a whiff.
'Tavern Brawl' the papers yell;
Let 'em rot in bloody hell.

They all got off, they always do,
The bastards never pay their dues.
No frills, no muck, just as it was;
We told you all this tale because
Our history is writ by winners-
But art and legend made by sinners.
Now we bid you all farewell,
We hope you didn't mind the smell.
Until we come across your way
Upon some other pleasant day,
Consider this: it hurts to tell.

All bow as Marlowe is carried through the curtains and offscreen. Fade to black.

The Edinburgh Lawyer

By Lesley-Anne Brewster

'Your trouble', opined my uncle, 'is, you've no sense of adventure. Laddies your age, back when I was your age, were more…more…'

'Adventurous?' I chanced.

'That same, but…' Pacing back and forth, as if to power the engine of his finer faculties, he opted for: 'More daring; daring, aye, and dauntless. They were bold, was what they were; made progress, that by any means. Bold. Whereas laddies these days are…well, backward-like at going forward; at advancing of their selves.'

'By any means, they are. But not by all,' I said 'If I am the case in point.'

'The case in point,' he said, deliberately, 'the case in point rests on yon depositions you've your elbow cocked on there. Which I might say took no small means upon my ain part to get hold on. So?'

I waited.

'You'll have read them?'

This was not a question, truly; and I had, in fact, read them. I could not, for any comfort, have done otherwise. He had slapped them down before me on the table in his chambers like a gauntlet, rising dust that smelled of wig chalk, claret, and stale pipe tobacco.

'So what think you? Is it likely in this day and age, a wizard?'

'I read 'warlock', rather. Here…' I showed the line, 'and more than once.'

He waved away semantics.

'Aye; but and howsoever cried, the panel here stands suspect, delate and defamed as guilty of the crimes of witchcraft and consorting wi the Devil. He is Is entitled under Scots Law to his counsel for defence.'

'Quite right and just,' I said, and so I truly thought. 'But given my seeming want of the adventurous sense, and retrograde ambitiousness…Why me?'

'Why…?' he was very nearly speechless. Very nearly, 'Do ye credit all yon business about wizardrie and witchcraft, do ye, Atholl?'

'No.' I thought about it. 'No.'

No more, my uncle took pains to assure me, did the vast majority of learned men. Not in this modern age, this eighteenth century, these self-professedly 'enlightened' times. He could foresee - indeed, he claimed to have sensed its slow establishment - a change in attitude which would undo the propagators of such persecutions; view their victims as deluded wretches more deserving of our pity than our prisons, come to laud their champions.

It was a case, an opportunity, become uncommon rare; and there was no doubt fame and silver to be wrung from sale of pamphlets and the like. For which the natural herd had an unnatural hunger…

There are gentlemen who speak, as it were, in flash flood; who can be no more diverted or dammed up against than that; the which besides, my uncle
was at that time Lord High Advocate.

I took the proffered brief.

The panel, termed in England the accused, was William Atherton, a smith incomer to the town of Bogmuir, someway westerly of Renfrew; in which burgh's Tollbooth he had lain some several weeks. The Depositions out of witnesses: his journeyman; three witches turned confessant; two neighbouring tenant farmers and, most tellingly, perhaps, the laird's third son and serving minister, portrayed him quite the man remarkable.
For charming beasts, and implements, for cursing them and folk besides, and notwithstanding frequent trysting with the Devil, I'd a wonder he had time to ply his trade.

But these were paper, men are flesh. Whilst Renfrew, it would seem, was unenlightened. So I was away to Lion's Close, to take my leave of Mistress Betty Forbes (of whom the more anon) and thence to saddle and away from Edinburgh, in the usual listless drizzle.

(Reader, I would recommend you never visit Renfrew; in especial, Renfrew tollbooth.)

My arrival being expected, I was at the first received into a mildewed upper chamber, there to be given a very mean glass of some sour red liquid matter and presented introduction to the several parties interested in the case:

The Lords Justiciar, pout-bellied all, and for the most part none too clean;

The local Presbyters, ranged cheery as a parliament of skulls;

And lastly, learned counsel for the prosecution, Master Andrew Grant of Elderslie

'Yon rain's the very plague,' he opened, 'trust it has not marred the sheen on your Del Rio.'

(He was here referring to *Disquisitionum Magicarum,* which, of all dreich tomes on witchery, was the favourite of Scotland, notwithstanding its having been penned by a Jesuit priest. I had bought mine in its latest edition, and keenly new, to cram from. No doubt but that his was tired from use.)

'In truth, I would not mind it wet.' I owned, 'I found it hellish dry.'
'As I this claret: claret, dry, d'ye see?'
'I...ah...'
He was, I saw at once, the sort who draws attention to, then titters at, his own wit. So I suffered his elucidating all there present, even as the rain dripped from my hems onto my boots; slid from my boots onto the boards.

'Good Master Grant,' I said, at last,' I must confess to being in no small haste to interview the panel. Therefore, sir, I pray you…'

'Certainly.' He danced aside. 'The turnkey and his henchmen - highland men, whose names escape me - should, by rights, be in the buckie by the stair foot.'

There indeed they were.

The office of turnkey does not, as a rule, much attract the finer stamp of man. Balbirnie, the incumbent in this instance, was a thorough classic, still; as grovelling deferential to myself as he was peremptory to his inferiors: great, lurking men, like scowling bearded apes, who caddied my possessions and myself down to the bowels of the building.

Where crouched Atherton; in darkness almost absolute and foulness startling even to a denizen of Edinburgh.

Jailers oftentimes misuse their tenants, notably those taint of witchcraft, out of fear, or else mistaken zeal; their usual methods being denial of that which most men would consider the necessities - sleep, victuals, blankets, and the like ; but in his naked flesh this man bore witness to less subtle cruelty.

(One night, when tottering drunken down the Netherbow, I happened on the remnant of a bear had dropped from out some baiter's wagon as he threw the turn. In Atherton, I saw its very shade.)

I stretched my hand forth, and he clasped it. His fingers were filthy beyond all description and stained black through yellow in time-layers of bruising, the flesh about the fingernails which yet remained a ragged, suppurating ruin.

'I am Stewart of Atholl. I am to be your advocate.' I said.

He fainted soundless in the straw.

My first endeavour was to offer surety on his behalf, as leaseholder and tradesman fully articled, that he would show before the Justices on two days lawful warning. Under pain of an amount I whittled, like a wife of Weem, down to some fourteen shillings Scots. Which sum being promised, he and I were freed, into the teeming rain.

He had no shoes; nor either would his shoes have fit, nor he been fit to walk in them. I was obliged, therefore, to shoulder him; then bundle him before me, with an arm about his rib cage, on my poor mare all the weary road to Bogmuir and his leasehold premises.

Where not a window showed intact.

That notwithstanding, all inside was neat enough. A slate-roofed workshop forge, whose chimney backed onto the sleeping chamber 'ben', and which, besides the means and items of his trade, contained a narrow pallet, two stools, and a bench on which I set my sheaf of books and papers down, preparatory to making start upon my argument.

I am not a natural philanthropist. I was myself soaked to the bone and, having drawn the shutters, needed light enough to read by, so I laid a fire. Then, since you cannot get warm eggs from out a cold hen (this a saying of my uncle's) set some water on to boil, and gathered up for Atherton such coverlets and garment cloths as I could find

'Grand lad, ye are, young Sir; a kind soul and a scholar. But for all,' he sighed, 'tis hopeless work you've here.'
'It is?' I asked but idly, being occupied, 'You are guilty of the charges?'
'No, I'm no' that.' he admitted.' Yet it's no light thing, this.'
'No.'

To be a smith takes strength of body. That his body, albeit deeply bruised and sadly torn about, had come intact from out of durance, spoke to that much; yet I worried for his mind.
'What I'm for saying is, a' your lawyer's arts, I cannot see them serve,' he said, 'they bound and pricked me, see you. Took a saddler's bodkin and... Balbirnie swore I'd parts as never bled.'
'And? You're a smith, man. Hide like horn. And I've a knack at this.' I told him. 'Now, your journeyman: how far into his time is he? And does the laird of Bogmuir own the leaseholds on both Barloch and Kilellan?'

There was much of fact as yet to ascertain, and I had bought myself but little time for such accomplishment. Besides which, Master Atherton - or, Will, as he had bid me style him- had no wish to be alone, and so he yielded up his cot to me and chose himself to occupy the pallet.
We were wakened, in the hollow of the night, to roars of:
'Warlock! Tyke! Hey, devil - come on oot ye, and get ended; else away and hang yoursel' and spare the burgh purse the fee!' and suchlike witticisms, to accompaniment of clattering of missiles, several hard, still others soft and farmyard pungent.
'They'll hae ma life ere they depart', Will moaned; not standing quite, for sake his hurts, but by some impulse of his own supported. 'They'll break doon the door and drag me oot, or else put torch to it, and see me burn...'
'Will you get down, Will! '
Even as I hissed this (yes, even in such grim predicament) I had to smile to catch myself at mouthing this.
'I have a pistol.'
That I did: a neat Italian flintlock, erstwhile property of Mistress Betty Forbes of Edinburgh. Which same, being noisily discharged, restored a silence.

I am hellish clever, roused.

All Scottish trials (Reader, in case you know not) are prefaced by an Air of Cause. A speech is made by counsel for the prosecution, then response made by the counsel for defence. Enlightened thus, the Justices confer to make a ruling on the relevance of the indictment. This indictment, naturally enough, supplies the ground for any verdict.

Master Andrew Grant, given audience, played gardener to the occult seeds therein, these being (his words) *Primus*: Witchcraft, and *Secondus:* Devil-worship. Nourished them with such ripe dung as he could rake from out the witness depositions, and then watered them with scripture, precedent, and quotes of pages out his library, which pages he had marked with trailing ribands; growing each to a rare tulip of dog Latin and hyperbole.

Myself, I stayed it short, but rose a thistle.

'Sirs, the Witchcraft Act of 1563,' I pointed out, 'upon which Act the several charges rest, is silent on the matter of addressing, meeting, and indeed, of worshipping, the Devil. It concerns those who consult with witches, or who practice witchcraft, nothing more. This much is borne out by the Books of Adjournal, in which all due proceedings are recorded.

Witches were condemned for making charms and laying enchantments, to the injury of those sufficient gullible to think them efficacious: all facts capable of proof; and therefore disproof.

But of trysting, sirs, and making compact with, the Devil, there is nothing. Not a jot. I move, respectfully, that the latter charge be deemed irrelevant to set before a jury.'

Such upset you never saw!

The Presbytery was on its heels; and Grant in haste to make objection, that for all he neither had one reasoned nor had right more than the ministers and elders to a hearing at this stage.

As for the Lords Justiciar, they were flummoxed.

If they erred, they did so on the side of caution.

'But we could not, do ye see, good sirs? We could not...'

Lord Blantyre, presiding, had no sooner stepped down from the bench of judgement than the self-elect of Renfrew mobbed him round. Milord endeavoured to be reasoned, even with his wig askew:

'We could not press a charge there is no law against.'

'Well, God amend the laws!' piped one; to much applause.

And, from another: 'Tis the Devil's work thou'rt at!'

(I fancied him the son of Bogmuir; and in that I was correct, as it transpired.)

'Thou shallt not profit thee thereby!'

So saying, he made direct for me, bearing a small book in his hand, likely a Bible, which he held up like a house brick. Drawing close to me, however, he was held back by the press about the bench; and somehow, in the tangle, caught my foot behind his ankle, which upended him entirely.

By-stepping his rescuers, I slipped Will and Blantyre out in my wake.

From all the tumult seen above, and from the charivari which had serenaded Will and I the night before, one might imagine all in Renfrew in an uproar, every burgess wild a-thirst for righteous vengeance. Yet in truth it was not so. Beyond the Tollbooth all stood quiet.

I could not see inside the houses, which faced gable-on the streets - these
loosely cobbled, where they were - for each was windowed low, else very high, deep-set and small. Nor could I, given the shawls and scowls and lowered hat brims steady rain necessitates, read anything of people's faces. They made wide way for each other; that I saw. Kept silence even between them selves, and went about their business.

'Going in dread,' was Will's word on it, 'stark a-feared they'll be attaint, and never mind the want o' cause. But I've apology to make you, for ye spoke me fair this day.'

I shrugged, and bent again to pistol-cleaning.

'They might have us on the other matter yet, mind, might they no'? I mean the witchery?"

'It's possible.' I owned, 'if scarcely rational. But not if I can help it.'

Will had somehow managed, from the remnants of his meal-kist and the ruin of his house-plot, to foment a barley brose. Had laced it with uisquebagh dark as fish oil, in my honour; and now lay back supping it with relish more than I could emulate, his awful fingers cupped about his bowl

'Say they should hang me yet…' he mused, 'at least, well, now they cannot hang me it twice.'

I swear I have never laughed so hard.

Yet it occurred to me I knew but little of him, this supposed man-witch, this warlock. In particular, knew nothing of his conduct in less rabid times, or any thing of what had made him target for the world's wrath, or at least that of John Semple, laird of Bogmuir. So I asked him. And he told me.

He was foreign to the place. Had habits, as might any man who lives alone,
were quite peculiar to himself. Once kept a lame dog for its company. Grew
wild mushrooms from the spore. But all the meat of any disputation with the minister hung on the fact that Will did not attend the Bogmuir kirk.

He told me why.

That in its time.

The morning after came in cold; and raining still. Behind it, word from Renfrew that the Lords Justiciar, no doubt now bowing to some pressure brought to bear upon them by the Burgh Session, had appointed date for trial. At the closest notice possible: Noon on the third day following.

There is an inn at Erskine ferry on the south bank of the Clyde; a cross-land mile or so from Bogmuir. This, a finer class of inn than any I had spied in Renfrew, found me inspiration, middling decent ale, roast beef, and oysters; which repast I shared with Will, by reason of his having shared his brose.

Flesh powers the reason (this, another saying of my uncle's) and I should say we were reasonable when we returned to Bogmuir. So full reasonable that, when the morning came, we found that we had fetched my mare inside with us, to dine upon the straw that lined Will's pallet.

Two days passed. I learned how uisquebagh is made. But to the trial :

Blantyre had found himself some business up in Glasgow, so his sheriff-depute, Lord Halcraig, was sitting. Will discerned for me John Semple, laird of Bogmuir, in the gallery in midst the Presbytery, he clad in velvets with a froth of lace, bestowing patrician looks upon the jury. Who were ranged like Sunday schoolboys at a cock-fight.

Renfrew's Burgh Bible is a yard across.

Before they may give legal testimony, every witness must be sworn in on a copy of The Testaments; that, once he has answered certain questions asked of him. To wit:

Has anyone instructed him on what to say?

Has he received any manner of benefit, or promise of benefit, from what he is about to say? And:

Does he bear malice against the accused?

These questions being answered in the negative, the witness raises up his right hand, showing the empty palm to all, and vows: 'The truth to tell and no truth to conceal, as he should answer in the Day of Judgement.' He is then described on record as: 'sworn purged of malice, prejudice and partial counsel.'

This is usually a swift formality. Consider, though, these witnesses; the questions which might reasonably be asked of them; and were.

Of Doig, Will's journeyman: 'Had he not earnings from the smithing he had done in his own right during the panel's long imprisonment? Were not those earnings monies to his benefit? And had he not the promise of inheriting his former master's custom?'

Of the tenant farmers, Barloch and Killellan: 'Was it not a curiousness indicative of partial counsel that they both, being bounden to the laird of Bogmuir – he whose son had brought the action – for their lease' continuance, had given their depositions to the secretary of that same, upon the same day, in the same place, and in presence of each other, using words identical? '

Of the confessants: 'They were witches, yes? Had freely, without use of force (at this Balbirnie slid his eyes away from mine, and those of other watchers) confirmed, owned, and admitted to as much? How might they then swear oath upon the Word?'

Here I was unexpectedly supported by the burgh dominie. Who dared them to do so and he'd see the Bible burn.

In short, they each and all had rendered themselves ineligible to be even sworn. This meant that the pursuant, Robert Semple M. A; serving minister to Bogmuir, stood alone as witness for the prosecution. And could he be truly said to bear no malice?

'I object, my Lord. I must and do, most strenuously.'
Poor Grant: with all his arrows broke bar one, he yet strove manfully to make a spear of it. In waiting, he had folded and re-folded elbows, knees, and bookmark ribands, scoured mud flecks from off his stockings with his thumbnail; now he stood with all his useless depositions crushed in one hand, showing a tremor in the inky other.

'My most learned colleague surely cannot mean by his last question to impugn the word or repute of a wearer of The Cloth?'

'Quite.' Lord Halcraig shifted his buttocks and frowned thunder down on me. 'Withdraw yon question, Atholl, ye blithe rogue, ye; and admit his bloody witness, for the patient love of God.'

'Even as you will, Milord.'

I bowed. To him; to Bogmuir, tinted like a beetroot boiled and straining at his stock; then, for round measure, to my counterpart. Who had begun to frown in puzzlement, and dart his glance between myself and Will and Will and I and Lord Halcraig; although he kept me in his eye even as his witness was sworn in to make sententious sermon of his testimony.

This was no less than his written deposition given voice. Had no more first-hand matter in it than that Will had never joined his congregation, nor been seen by him between sun's setting Saturday and first light of a Monday.

'From which fact you did infer,' fed Grant, 'the evil influence and malicious workings of some occult, supernatural agency?'

'I did, indeed: a league with death, and covenant with Hell!'

Here Grant, in guise of exposition, gave some tedious account of how invisibility might be accomplished with the preternatural aid of demons. Then, drawing out his corrugated places from Del Rio, he discoursed at length on why it likely was the case that witches dared not enter onto sacred ground.

Since he was doing my case no real disservice - half the jury had been left behind long since, and even Milord was yawning - I allowed him stale the air. Asked in my own turn:

'So you say you did not see the accused?'

'No, that I did not; not between the hours here aforesaid' replied the minister, quite calmly.

'And myself, Sir?' I enquired. 'Was I remarked or witnessed by your self at any point, on Friday evening, or on Saturday, or yet this Sunday past? Have you in fact laid eyes upon me since the last occasion of our meeting in this very court?'

'Not as I can recall.' he said, 'which is to say, I have not. No.'

'And from that much you would deduce that, in the interim, I had gone invisible?'

I turned my back on him and looked all smiling pity to the jury, some of whom laughed in their sleeves, or out aloud.

'No. No. I would not that. But it is fact well known that witches hold their naughty gatherings, their sabbats, of a Friday night, and take their rest the Saturday. Moreover, this was week on week, and no-one ever saw him.'

'No-one saw him who was known to you.' I pointed out, 'so, since he had not joined your own assembly, you surpassed your own deductions and adjudged him apostate?'

'I did. I do, aye. That, and worse yet…'

He, like Grant, was fairly bursting to spew forth all his assembled evidence: the dog, which, in a manifest perversion of the sacred rite of baptism, had been given a name; the conjuring of mushrooms out of ground where they had not been known to grow; the copper vessel, redolent of alchemy, which sat for days upon the forge flames; all the instances of seeming mischance which had followed quickly, else eventually, on from some encounter with the outland smith. But these, from his lips, were mere hearsay, therefore not admissible in evidence.

'I have nothing further of this witness.' I admitted. 'But, Milord, if I may beg indulgence to call forth to oath one whose sworn testimony should shed light upon the matter of the panel's where about…'

'You've got a witness?' Grant gasped. 'Who…?'

I had secured Milord's consent, and so:

'I call the Reverend Doctor Alexander Milne, commissioner for Strathblane.' I said, then skipped aside to give my witness leave to pass; and all the court the same to wonder.

Where the godly men of Renfrew to a one looked like a decent diet of meat would be beyond their expectation, Milne was built on my uncle's scale. He sailed in fronted by a belly clad in black sateen, his full wig balancing a quite tremendously empurpled nose and diverse folds of rosy jowl; to make his legal declaration with the air of one who, on the Day of Doom, fully expects to ease his ample self onto the Justice bench.

Aye, William Atherton was known to him. He'd christened him, by God. And did not that same Christian soul take ferry o'er the Clyde and walk a score of miles to hear the sermon in his own home parish? Had he not at times to bed him down upon

Kilpatrick braes, moreover, some fool having thought best to anticipate the Lord and start the timing of the Sabbath from
the evening of the Saturday ?
Will had no case to answer.

    'Well? Adventurous sufficient, do you think?' I asked my uncle.

    'Hmm…' His praise was ever given in apothecary doses. 'Aye; but yet you might have sought for reparation after slander, defamation…'

    'So I might have. Save that Atherton expressed to me his wish for nothing more than to be settled back in Strathblane.'

    'You'll be glad to be returned to Edinburgh, yourself.'
About to say that certainly the change of rain was welcome, I caught notice of his tone. Asked: 'Why do you say so?'

    'Mistress Forbes has been detained upon a charge of harlotry...'

(That, naturally, is quite another tale. But even the above is not quite yet this story's end. Permit me, reader, quote you here a passage from Beale's volume of 'Traditions and Quaint Tales concerning Renfrew':

    'Legend round the burgh proper has it that in that same year, being the sixth year of Gorge second (ie 1752), the Devil, donning aspect of an Edinburgh lawyer, by his cunning and his glamour won a warlock free the Tollbooth

The Sennachie in: The Keek Stane

A Crime Uncommon

By Lesley-Anne Brewster

The end beginning. Every closed case comes to this: a cold wait in a High Court corridor. Like Limbo, with a drinks machine.
  DS Cargill – his friends, if he had friends, would call him Linden – rubs his palms along his thighs. He has legs like a runner; the hands of a concert pianist; a blue suit, unremarkable. No life.
  Just work.

He had been eating cold pakora when the call came in. The first one: Marta Devlin: IC1; blonde; forty-seven; no convictions. Very dead.

Despite what people think, cold-blooded murder is a crime uncommon. Few police personnel will ever see it. None become inured to it.
  DC MacLellan had thrown up – God love him, outwith the immediate scene; whilst DC Ullikummi, with her usual poise, barked, snarled and snapped back any uniform who might have otherwise contaminated same, sending them off to canvass houses, nearby businesses. What ever.
  The pathologist, the SOCOs with their handheld lights and cameras, the techies and the squad from Fingerprints, had come and busied round and gone and left Cargill alone with Marta.
  Then he had been left alone with Janis; then with Evelyn, known as 'Evie'; then with Kate; then ' Tish' ; then Barbara-Anne; then Lauren.

Left there, looking. Staring at the scene, the corpse, as though it were a piece of installation art; a source to glean for textures, deeper meanings. Why this woman, and why here, not in her bedroom? Given the knife blows, why the ligature? (mere over-kill?) So: why the pose? What did he add, and what did he omit ? What was he trying to say about the victims; trying to say to the police, or to the world in general?
  What was the artist thinking here?

Cargill had sketched them in his notebooks. Marked the original locations of each stick of furniture, each scrap of evidence recovered. Any item that seemed out of place, seemed not to fit with its surroundings, he examined.

He would amass reports on fibres, fluids. Wound casts. Sort through screeds of reminiscences from those who knew the victims, had been married to the victims, lived beside them, worked beside them, ate beside them, slept beside them.
  And the first would give him nothing. He had heard the explanations. Knew how difficult it was to lift a fingerprint from flesh. Knew that, dependant on their individual biochemistry, at peak arousal many people do not leave a print, and easily more than

half the nation's males do not conveniently secrete their DNA into their body fluids, either.
Real life isn't telly: trace lab rarely makes a case.

The DCs Ullikumi and MacLellan (bad cop, worse cop) had come up with NDL on victim backgrounds. They were not Linked; at least, Not Discernibly. Cargill had re-read every line of their reports and found no fault, except with Jim MacLellan's spelling.
People lie to the police. The criminals are, naturally, obliged to. Witnesses, should they come forward or be winkled out, almost invariably do, whether
intentionally or no. Memory is selfish: if it doesn't touch on you, it isn't likely to leave much of an impression. By comparing their accounts to what the crime scene tells you, you can usually find out the full extent of their invention; but most ordinary members of the public, choose to filter what they say, assess it for acceptability. Don't like to speak an ill word of the damaged or the dead.

'QC's a bastard.'
Ullikumi, having given her evidence, has been disgorged amidst a clutch of lawyer's clerks. She is pretending to be talking to the first of these, a sorry-looking nose drip, name of Tontine. Cargill thinks it strange to see her in a skirt, earrings and heels.
He nods; studies the floor tiles. Likely late Victorian, he decides. Tontine returns. His shoes, black brogues, are cracked from want of polish.
'Can I get you anything?' he asks.
'A thermal blanket?'
'Haha. Yes. It's quite...' Tontine, happed up in woollen wig and gown, smiles like a hopeful undertaker. '...chilly. Yes, I daresay. Still, it shouldn't be too long now...'
'No.'
Denied the pleasantries of closing, Tontine lingers, then departs.
Cargill sinks back into remembrance.

He had been stumped. They all had. Seven women dead, and not one useful lead. The Press- the tabloid press, at least -were loving it; going large on every detail of whatever nonsense they could get their hands on. Had paid two grand out to Kate's boss (bloody-fingered Kate, who had fought until her nail beds tore)for copies of the photographs attached to her personnel file, and some muck about her Socialist sympathies.
As if the Task Force: operation codename Cutter, nominally under DI Stark, who bounced between the Top Brass and Cargill and Forman's bands of malcontents: had not explored even that dim cul-de-sac.

Forget the notion of epiphany; of something 'clicking into place' in one brief, righteous moment. In the real world, no detective, amateur or otherwise, will find the one clue, make the one connection, which unlocks the case.

You take what you are sure of, and you run with it, in the most promising direction, then the next, and then the next. And all the while, you are exquisitely conscious of the passing minutes, hours, days, weeks (each costed by the Service) which your villain spends Scot-free. Time he has severed, amputated, from his victims.

How investigating officers with friends and family cope, DS Cargill cannot imagine. He could barely bring himself to grunt at newsagents and neighbours. Took to dressing, showering in the dark; avoiding any sight of flesh.

Approximately eight of every hundred murders will remain unsolved. Of these, a high percentage is of high-risk victims, prostitutes and homeless people, in the main, killed by a careful stranger. Just occasionally, that stranger will, from some compulsion best known to himself and highly-paid psychologists, go on to kill again. The second time, he might be caught. If he has been less careful: has been seen, or heard to boast, or thought to hold on to some keepsake, or (it happens, albeit seldom) has confessed, it may be possible to link him to the original murder. May be.
    In the other ninety-two, the saving grace of the investigating team is that a killer, just like any other criminal, is predisposed toward incompetence, or at the least, toward error.

Skill at murder is not easily acquired. And so...

Doors open on another court, one further down the corridor. A crowd in Sunday clothes is hushed by ushers; herded toward another exit. Some form cabals round the pillars. Cargill listens idly to the muted murmuration, punctuated by the occasional throat-clearing cough or click of heels. He feels the slyly curious glances lobbed in his direction.
    He avoids eye contact. Always.
After a time, he rise; with a tendon click in one knee. Mines his pockets for the sixty pence he needs to buy a coffee hot enough to warp the cup; carries it gingerly: a trial by ordeal.
    He sits back down.

They had known, and the profiler engaged to put a jargon-laden seal on it agreed, that they were chasing the senseless red trail of a psychopath. Nobody seeing the bodies could have doubted it. Hence the informal designation : 'Operation Nutter '.
    Thank you and goodnight, Jack Forman.

Cargill knew that, whether born or made (that jury was still out, as far as he had heard) a psychopath does not just leap from being your normal citizen to executing mutilation murder. He might wear a mask of sanity, but only loosely.
He: the bulk of them were men: was never truly normal.

He could have no conscience; no compassion. No ability to comprehend such abstract terms as truth, love, or the future. His was madness *in excelsis*. But he had to have started small.

And so Cargill, no longer putting in for overtime he knew would be denied, went hunting petty crimes; the more seemingly motiveless and violent the better. Geographics, charting the locations of the victims, had come up with a projected 'safe zone': even killers only travel so far, seldom dirty their own doorsteps. Uniform had been all over it, but only in connection with the murders.

Surely somebody in there had scented lion.

Danny North. The name kept coming up. The old wife with the Rich Tea biscuits had been terrified; the corner yobs in awe. There was nothing spectacular on North's record: couple of break-ins, minor time, and three domestics. Hints of several others dropped. Cargill noticed that the complaints had come from different complainants, two of, to be exact; and he could find no sign of either of them.

'Flitted out.' the old wife thought.

Maybe.

But both stopped drawing benefit? No. No chance. Armed with nothing more than that, and information gleaned from talking to the taxman, who considered it unlikely both had found illegal work or won the Irish Lottery, Cargill went in to DI Stark.

Stood silent through the bollocking and waited for the nod.

'Wee shite got cocky.' Stark opined. 'Have Ullikumi keep an eye on him, for he'll get ikey at a lassie. Put MacLellan and,...ach, what's his name, that specky lad o Forman's?'

'DC Greig.' Cargill supplied.

'Get that pair...ach, get anyone that's handy...sifting through the dross that was lifted at the scene before we file the docket for a search o premises. Forman can draft it- he's got the knack for paperwork. He can get reading through the statements, too. See if there's ony mention of your boy. And you can chase it down the other road. See if we can work out how they other women,our known victims, crossed the path o Danny North. It would be handy if we found the other pair, mind.'

Handy, aye.

Nine women: seven killed inside their homes, two possibly in North's own flat.
There could be more.

He had obviously stopped hiding them; had happened on the thrill of linking pastimes. Neither simply breaking in on other people's private living space, nor wounding women to the point of death and further, had sufficed him after Marta Devlin.

Hers had been a neat house: nothing dirty, nothing out of place; the plants well-watered, somehow warm and welcoming. Much like the woman was in life, by all accounts. The kind of woman he, Cargill, would love to know, but never had the slightest prospect of attracting. Opposites repel.

But what was it about her, or the others, that had drawn North's rage?

A psychopath is fuelled by rage, unthinking rage; and repetitive, self-elaborating fantasy. He is a liar, and not a good one; since to tell a decent lie, you have to care to be believed. To him, his victims stand for something other than themselves; are merely objects, putty figures, cut-outs of his monsters: those who crossed him, caught him lying, burst his bubble of conceit.

When they had North, Cargill would ask him.

When they did, when close surveillance by Ashandra Ullikumi had provoked North into viciousness they could arrest him for, and they could search the pit he lived in, there were blood stains on the walls. Those could be typed; and were, although that took days, not the seconds it does in the movies; and cost the Police Service a packet, besides. But in the end, it was 'found to cohere with a high probability' with Sandra Thane's, and Diane Horseburgh's, and conveniently, if curiously, with Evie Wright's.

Three down.

While three would be enough to see North put away for life, it hadn't quite sufficed Cargill. He had insisted on a face-to-face.

And that had brought him here. To this chill corridor, the Gents a lengthy walk away, the coffee pressing at his bladder.

Moving rapidly, and flinching at the coldness of his hands, he paid a hasty call on nature, though he hated public toilets. Always fancied there was someone watching; knowing that there so often was. He only hoped he would be back seated on the uncomfortable bench before they thought to call him.

Quickly, quickly: no-one there.

It is a source of constant disappointment to detectives, as to members of the public, to discover just how commonplace most murderers look. They could be anyone. They are.

They are also generally, boring, even dull in conversation; shallow, self-obsessed and vain; and, for the most part, poorly educated, since, to learn, you have to first admit that you don't know.

There are few, if any, Doctor Lecters.

Nor is there much scientific method to interrogation. Even in the presence of their counsel, the majority of criminals endeavour to explain themselves, to justify their conduct.

Virtually every one imagines they can come up with the magic formula: part alibi and part excuse of provocation, which will win the stupid world round to their so-superior view of things, their absolute, unblinking way of thinking. See them home. All that a skilled interrogator has to do is let them play the rope out, and then draw it into a noose.

But Danny North…
    The first thing anyone would notice is how perfectly symmetrical his face is; and how handsome. How he is muscled like a working god, his hair well cut, his teeth bright-polished, though his clothes were scruffy, more than slightly stale. Should he elect to move while they are watching him (his customary stillness is remarkable) they cannot but be stunned by his quick economy of motion. And contrast his eyes and voice…

To hear him was like seeing the Trevi fountain spout wet filth.

He gave, in detail, all they needed to convict him for the murders of the nine; then he gave more. He said he had hanged a man, his cell mate, when in prison, made it look like suicide; had knifed to death a homeless couple, then set fire to them; and even boasted that he had burned the corpses of his former 'shack-ups', Sandra and Diane.

And why? because he could; because he felt like it.

At last.
    '*DS Cargill ! Detective Sergeant Linden Cargill to Court one, please.*'
    Tontine. Looking constipated.
    '*Here.*'
    Cargill stood as his name was ticked off on the shabby clipboard, as the left side of the double doors was parted just enough to ease him in. He caught a brief glimpse of MacClellan, Greig and Forman on the sidelines like a trio of football coaches. Feeling that damn knee twinge again, he took the stand; the Christian version of the oath.
    Swore by Almighty God to tell the truth; and did, and for a moment, felt a touch of triumph, of closure.

Then he met North's eyes. Saw North was smiling, and could se, behind the smile, an easy certainty that there was evil still to do. Read in it North's intent to choose his time of dying; and die by his own hand. Not as the easy, or the coward's way, but as the ultimate control trip.
    Cargill could not let that happen.

So he nodded, almost casually, to someone in the gallery. A someone who was someone in the criminal fraternity; a someone whom he might have owned as friend, had not the Service such a dim view of such friendships. And that someone nodded back.

FRAGMENTATION: King John to Prince Arthur of Brittany

By Lesley-Anne Brewster

Go wary of kings when they start to build churches. My father Henry was a great
    church builder; and the world, and most especially Saint Tom Beckett,
knows what manner stainless soul he had.
       He never was a bugger, though. Unlike our lion-hearted Richard, who was so-named for his pride in acquisition, never anything of valour, as it happens. Still, the dead are sanitised by time; else filthied, in its passage. Much depends on how their rivals fare; which enemies outlast them.
       There were miracles at Beckett's tomb, and sodomites in mourning webs at Richard's funeral. And, as I rode here, whistling golden under this green morning, I heard voices from the wild wood whispering 'Mordred' after me, as if they had somehow wised my purpose. Mordred: who, of course, was good King Arthur's slayer; and his nephew, in the gestes. So course the minds of Englishmen. Although their tangled tongues so maul words, I suppose it may have been meant for 'murder', even 'murderer'.
       The woods, you know, are rife with wolfsheads. Which is something I, as king, intend to address; besides the church men; and the churches which I do not mean to build, yet. Not unless it be in oak, to fell all shelter from the outlaws; else in miniature, as subtleties in almond paste and sugar. Once I retake lands were lost to me by my unsubtle need to battle you at Mirabeau.
       And yet my plans beyond this moment, nephew, rival, Arthur, are not your concern. Anjou and Aquitaine support you, but I never was my royal mother's favourite; nor my father's. Although Richard, Richard liked me over well…

Should I then dedicate a chapel to your memory?

Old Frog

By Chaz Wood
Illustration by Frang McHardy

Old Frog sat on the marsh's border, the line between the flyswarming murk and the lush grassblowing freedom of the field.

He was too old, too old to leap, too old even to feed himself now.

He had been around too long, from the old and far-gone days when he sang *brek krek krek koaxkoax* and was the toast of emperors and priests, the muse of poets. But he sang little now, nor did he hear much in the way of singing, for his people had long abandoned this corner of the world. There was only him, him alone, among a multitude of strange species who may or may not be friendly, or edible.

He was Old Frog, he was the first, he told himself again. The distant dragonfly song of zzziiimmm zzzooomm zzzuumm recalled younger days when he would have been across the pond in a single leap, and the bold and haughty dragonfly, no more. Even the Kingfisher looked lazily away, as though such a prey was hardly worth his effort. Kingfisher would snap the dragonfly in his own time, knowing that Old Frog had no chance of beating him to it.

He had starved now for three days, and would soon be dead. Too old, too stiff…too old to live, too tired to find out who among these buzzing and splishing alien things could feed him, or kill him. He would die soon then, from thirst or hunger, and become crowfood. He hated those black feathercocks, their bloody beaks, their dirty dark voices. They never had to sneak up on their prey, or sit motionless shuddering from hunger, waiting for the precise moment to strike. Not for them cunning, stealth, skill. Just the old, the sick, the dead, to be pecked and pulled.

But no, that was not how it would be. Crow's brood would never feast on Old Frog, never. He would return to the water that birthed him before he would allow that.

The dragonfly taunted him, buzzing him, its wings wafting him. Challenging Old Frog in his own element, challenging his very origins, laughing at his credentials. Nobody lived now who could tell of the old and far-off days when Old Frog could snap a hundred flies from the sky before breakfast, when of course he wasn't so Old, when not a dragonfly nor a serpentfly was safe from his lethal tongue, and when he knew every lilypad within that flyswarming murk and the shortest route from anywhere to anywhere else was but a swift bound.

He felt the tingling in his legs, the sensation he always got before a jump, a kill, a meal. He tautened, feeling his skinny bones tremble as he knew they would. The will wasn't lacking; the body was. It had been a harsh three days.

He opened wide his throat to the sky, and called to all: "I am Old Frog, I was keeper of this marsh in the old and far-gone days. I am King of the Lilypad and evermore shall be!"

And the dragonfly buzzed in its laughter, and the marsh belched with disbelief. Kingfisher blinked, and pondered his next move. Old Frog had spoken;

clearly he was waking up. Kingfisher considered snapping the dragonfly soon before foolish Old Frog failed to do so, and scared the thing away completely.

Old Frog sensed – didn't see – just felt - the flurry of feathers from the riverbank. Kingfisher was stirring, considering his chances with the dragonfly against Old Frog.

Now Old Frog knew. He had spoken, now he must act.

And in a eruption of electric energy, his legs launched him skyward – he was leaping, the marsh flashing beneath him, and just for a moment – a *moment* – he saw the dragonfly freeze in mid-air with disbelief, just before the legendary Old Frog tongue unfurled, unseen for so long. Kingfisher screamed and fluttered in his panic as the shadow of Old Frog blacked out his view of the dragonfly, and Old Frog continued to darken the sky of those beneath him through his incredible leap. For he *was* Old Frog, keeper of the marsh, the fluswarming murk, in the old and far-gone days. And he *was* King of the Lilypad.

For in that moment, the marsh held its breath as the old song *brek krek krek koaxkoax* rang once more in his ears, and the dragonfly hummed with terror beneath the lethal tongue of Old Frog.

Cerulean Blue

By Lesley-Anne Brewster

'Gali-who?'
'Galahad.'
The intensely beautiful young blond man smiled, sharpening his beauty to a point almost beyond believable. That smile made Caterina blush; made her forget that she was doomed, that life was ten times worse than merely bad; made Chelsea Bridge diminish into insignificance.

His eyes were cerulean blue.

'I...thanks, I think.' What more was there to say to someone who had just caught you on the verge of jumping from a parapet?
The Thames surged on below them both; swirled round the uprights of the bridge like angry coffee. Filthy angry coffee, greyed about the foam with ash, and not at all enticing.

She felt curiously relieved; curiously calm and, even more curiously, hungry. Round the corner by the junction with the Nine Elms Road there was a Greasy Spoon where they did fry-ups that would give you heart disease. She reckoned she could stand her rescuer a cup of brew, at least.

'Is that your real name?'
'Yes.'
He did not look offended; had not told her any more about himself, or asked her why she had been about to do what she had been about to do, or anything. She liked that. Liked the scent of him; the way he walked, the way he sat, straight-shouldered but relaxed; the way the winter sunlight lit his hair sort of like Colgate toothpaste's 'ring of confidence'.

She almost smiled to see the way the waitress looked at him like he was on the telly then stared, marvelling, at her, before licking a blue-edged thumb to turn over the sheet of carbon paper in her notepad.

'Tea for me, please; and...' She turned to him, asked: 'tea or coffee?'
He looked blank.
'Hot chocolate then, or Bovril? Maybe Coke? Sprite?' She was close to the foot of the limited 'beverages' menu, but 'Galahad' seemed to have an
unlimited supply of vacant looks. '...Milk?'
'Milk?'
'D' you...would you like a glass of milk?'
'Yes. Thank you. Milk.'
He grinned.
'And two...' She reckoned she could eat it if he didn't, and could just afford it: 'two Full English Breakfasts.'

She had never tasted food so good. Well, not since Joe died. Not since they had told her that she had it, too: The Virus. Not the full-blown thing, but the potential to develop it. Those were the words they had used. 'Develop it., as if it was a spool of film, a set of rotten photographs.

The day light was so bright now that it picked out the old thumbprints on the thick glass cups, the shadows of the toast crumbs. Made spilt egg yolk look so yellow that it almost hurt her heart to look at it. She looked away; and was shocked into wonder by the absolute perfection of the painted flowers on a toddler's wellies.
    'It is beautiful and precious, is not?' asked Galahad.
    'What is?'
    'The moment. Now. The World. Creation manifest.'
    'Oh.'

He was one of those. She should have guessed it, really, from the milk. So any minute now he would get the pamphlets out: selected texts in snippets from some bright, castrated Bible, with the address of the nearest house of Christian worship stamped in smeared ink at the bottom.
    'I suppose so.'
    'You had Faith once.'
    'Did I? I suppose I did,' she said. 'But that was long ago.' She put her loaded fork down. Found his eyes again: those awesome, guileless eyes.
    'It was a child's faith, and it failed me.'
    'Truly?'
    'Really.' She said. 'Really and truly. Yep.'
But somehow that was not enough. She did not want to talk about herself, she never did. She had heard too much of other people's mewling 'It's not fair... why me?' at the support group. Joe, who had been shattered at the start, but toward the end stayed strong, so strong, had tried to shut them up by asking them: 'Why not you?'

And yet here she was now, suddenly, relating the entire grim story of her life and love, her anger, hopes and disappointments, to an almost total stranger. To the only man she had ever seen who actually looked seriously handsome with a milk moustachio.
    'Nobody cares.' she said, at last.
    'Do you?'
She thought that over.
    'No. At least, I didn't.. Just before you caught me, caught a hold of me, I sort of started to. Survival instinct, I suppose. I really loved Joe; really loved him. So I cared for him, and cared about him. But I don't...I never really liked myself, although I did my best. I did.'
    Realising that was like a knot unwound down someplace deep inside her belly. Like the quiet after weeping, or a long drink of cold water at a hot, hard journey's end.

Caterina noticed that she wasn't angry any more; or even scared. She was just sad; and only vaguely sad, at that.

'Suppose now you're going to tell me that God loves me.'
He said nothing.

'What's your story, then? I've told you mine.'
'You know me not?' he asked, and smiled, but wistfully.
'I...No, how could I? We've only just met.'
Then she began remembering...a painting from so long ago; from long before the sad days, all the shadowed, dying days. A sunlit painting hanging in a gallery: a kneeling knight in armour, by Burne-Jones, maybe. His face....the legend...

'But you can't...You don't mean...really Galahad? Sir Galahad, the son of Lancelot, the one who found the Holy Grail? You mean you think you're him'
'I am. He.' he said, gently. 'Yet it was not given me to find the Grail. That honour was accorded to the one who was the best of us. Sir Constantin, styled Pursuival, the follower. He had such simple Faith - a child's faith. Whereas I...', he sighed, ' but won a sight of it; a sight of Heaven. Yet so full sweet was that to me, that all the mortal world thereafter seemed but empty, flat and stale. And so I laid me down to die, and die I did. My will was even so strong as that, to countermand the very Urge of God'.

'If you don't mind my saying so,' Caterina said, 'you seem to have talked yourself out of the story. But go on.'

He smiled.
'I did.'
'What?'
'I went on. Not to oblivion; nor yet to Paradise, where there is only...God.'
Lifting the paper napkin out from underneath his glass, he folded it and wiped his lips, his perfect lips, with it.

'I saw my life.' He said. 'Each moment, even as it was; like to a light held glancing to the planes and facets of a wondrous crystal. And I loved it, loved the immanence of deity in the unfolding of Creation, till my soul sang Love, and I became what I am now become.'

'Which is?' she asked, although she thought she knew.
'I am a messenger.'
'An angel? You're my guardian angel, is that what you're saying?'
'Not that.'
'No? What, then? Tell me. Galahad...'
'I am a messenger; a courier, if you will. I go to gather to The Light those souls in whom free will is manifest as wasteful impulse to self-murder. Where I may, I seek to wake in them some sorrow for their loss; some love of all that is, and was, and ever shall be. Try to win them to forgiveness and acceptance of themselves; since lacking that, they are doomed out of their own minds, and I cannot free them rise.'

' So...are you saying what I think you're saying?' she said; and realised that it didn't matter; that it never had. She'd done her best, and loved, and she still did. 'You never rescued me? I'm...

Mouse

By Lesley-Anne Brewster

> 'Mouse, Mouse, go back to your house
> Your daughter's a strumpet
> who's pimping your spouse!'

I looked up from a vague contemplation of my boot-tips and the cobbles underfoot to see Kit Marlowe, glittering like a dust mote, grinning ear to ear. I smiled, because he was my friend; and because Marlowe, with his merry fallen-angel face, was God-created to be smiled upon. I heel-trundled along as he fell in beside me, beginning a discourse on the topic of breakfast, in two contrapuntal voices.

Six months earlier I had arrived in Wittemberg from Cambridge (like Marlowe) to study Divinity (again like Marlowe) and been welcomed by him as effusively as the Lyconians welcomed Jupiter. I had spent much time thereafter in his company; accomplishing but little in the way of study as result, yet learning much, for all. He had chosen me as foil, the dark against the which his lights might all the brighter shine; and never was there a more ill-matched pair than me with my vast height, my head full of Hebrew and Greek, my tongue snagged by a spitting stutter, and Kit Marlowe, a deft humming-bird in scarlet high-heeled boots.

' ...to say that were the final statement on the subject, then the house has come down all in favour of a rousing ' Aye ', with even the very founds agreed to repair forthwith to a tavern, if such an alien creature might be flushed from covert in the precinct of this bilious, seething town. What mind yours, Rilke ? '
    I shrugged, then nodded.
'The ayes have it! Amytas, lend me your arm...' He took it unresisting prisoner. 'We shall feast upon the fruits of labours yet undone; and if we are undone therefore, at least we'll hang the heavier for it's sake. All though I do heartily crave good beef in this foul land of fried flour, boiled flour, baked flour, mackerel, veal and mutton livers. God's cods, how I hate this country! '
    'You love it when not hating it.' I said, just as soon as my tangle-rooted tongue allowed the words twist past.

It was, and is, my custom to be spare of speech, for reasons obvious. One cause, then, of my liking Kit so well was that he never would anticipate me as most folk are quick to do, from commonplace impatience or misguided altruism. He beamed at me.
    'True. I am a man much given to extremes.'

We walked on a while in silence made companionable by our closeness, as the city of Wittemberg awoke about us; in an unwinding sunlit flurry of market-booth assemblage, hopeful beggars, swinging water-bearers, and stray curs. Rounded a corner, entering one of the myriad extremely similar squares which, patched uneven at the seams, comprise the place.

Were passing by a saddler's heavy with the cloying reek of leather, when Marlowe startled; tugged my arm. Hissed:

'Run!'

I ran. Down narrow alleys overhung with linens draped to dry, and over gutters thick with rot; through vennels where my high head barely skimmed the curling plaster; over bridges where his heels rang out flat clarion.

Pressing past the mobs which gathered to scold roups, to steer deliveries of furniture or produce, or to take some worldy lesson from the slow exeunt of coffins or the spectacle of public penances, I ran; and Marlowe ran; and somehow we kept virtually apace, though once or twice he slipped my sight, which startled my bird-bellows heart to thudding all the wilder in its cage of heaving ribs. And all the while I felt our hunters closing ever in; and all the while I wondered who they were.

I knew they could be none of mine. Pedantic, I met credit promptly, gave way in the street, and seldom said enough to give offence. So, to my knowing, I had not a single foe in all the world. Kit Marlowe, on the other hand...

He lived far and away beyond even his scarce slender means. Could never stay a newly-minted slander if it seemed too sweetly apt; and was (I had seen it) prone to suffering the entire romantic cycle from first courtship to infatuation, consummation, disaffection and repugnance three or four times quarterly, with partners out of either sex.

Was this a creditor, or irate spouse? A disaffected lover; else some bravo he had bested in a duel? For he could fight, and oft times did. Perhaps a worthy of the Jesuit College, angered at some atheistic satire he had wrought? Or someone come from England, where his case was criminal, say infamous at least? I had heard him speak of Raleigh and his School of Night; heard him speak equally of Walsingham...

He had sworn me to silence; that without the slightest hint of a self-conscious irony. There would be chosen men, he had said; cold-blooded, wild, audacious men, whose every crime, even murder, would be sanctioned in their country's cause. Which men, whose days would naturally, be numbered; would themselves be numbered, even as he was numbered; and his number cipher: zero zero one.

I strove to keep him in my eye. Succeeded only in half-turning to collide against a short cheese-seller's prentice, whose tray corner caught me square above the ear. Neat-columned gold-waxed rounds rose in the air like coins thrown to the crowd at weddings.

Trailing my apologies, I loped away. Cupping my hand about that side my head until we reached a fountain square where Marlowe, looking back, saw blood splay out between my parted fingers; slid hard to a skittering halt.

'What…? Rilke, my man, your head's tapped claret. How so? '

Given the need to bathe my broken head; my breathlessness; and my frustrating tendency to false-start, gag, repeat and falter on the initial syllables of 'corner', 'cobbles', 'cheese' and even 'tray', it took me no small time to tell him.

Even then, I had more urgency to know if we were free of our pursuit; and not a deal less to be wise of their identity.

'Ah-ha. '

His green eyes soared seraphic upward. He ground his peculiarly small white teeth against his pouting lower lip. Then did a curious shuffle-jig which sent him out beyond my arm's reach.

'No-one, actually,' he said.' I simply took a fancy, like an hawk un-jessed, for sudden furious flight.'

Already dredged for words, I found I had none.

So I simply stood there. Stared agog at him as (needs must grant him that slight grace) he blushed. So much for his audacious men; I thought; and so much for his scarcely-enigmatic cipher!

Then, struck by sheer relief, and the utter nonsensicality of what had taken place, I laughed. And Marlowe laughed; his laughter like a descant peal of bells. And we embraced. And then I dropped him in the fountain.

The Labourer's Hire

by

J. I. Stuart

Prologue

By the middle of the twenty-seventh century AD, the Terran Empire, held together by a dominant and extensive navy, and underpinned with colonial tribute from over seven thousand daughter planets had got so far above itself that it had deliberately precipitated a bloody war against those two alien cultures nearest to it in size and development - the Chorae and the Alanyi.

The senseless killing and destruction, the rape and violence raged for years, and Terra had been slowly gaining the upper hand when suddenly, in a single instant, a freak million-to-one cosmic accident changed everything: an anti-matter asteroid streaking into the Terran home system at the speed of light actually struck Earth, and the force of the resultant detonation virtually wiped out the entire system. The far flung and overtaxed Empire, suddenly deprived of its head, collapsed inwards upon itself, with most of its technology lost, whilst the late opponents thankfully disbanded their armed forces and started to rebuild their shattered worlds and works.

Dating from about this time also, can be recorded early encounters with the Klylii, that enigmatic people, technologically so far ahead of all other known races; or rather, first sightings of their vast spaceships. From the confused stories of the period, it is hard to distinguish fact from fantasy, for tales suggesting that the Klylii fought both against the Empire, and assisted humans in distress seem to contain equal validity.

Be that as it may, over the succeeding centuries, whilst the Galaxy recovered from the war, and evolved into the state we know today, stories of the Klylii and their works continued to increase in number, type and degree. Indeed the quality and quantity of impeccably documented evidence early on reached such proportions that not even the most hardened skeptics dared deny the Klylii's actions. Some of them, it is true, challenged the Klylii motives for their selfless acts of charity, denying that true altruism was possible, or indeed desirable, but these were isolated criticisms lost in the sea of wonder and gratitude engendered by the fantastic actions of a race that today, is truly worshipped by over half civilized space as gods. And if a God is one who performs miracles to save unfortunates doomed to death through no fault of their own, why then, the Klylii are indeed, the Gods.

Unchallenged, unknown, the Klylii go their own mysterious way. They could have ruled all space with an iron hand, but instead choose to wander as space gypsies giving aid and assistance to all, as and when needed.
The race that could, in reality be said to rule space is, in fact, the pitied remnants of the once despised, proud and cruel Human Empire. In their purchased, hired, or leased ships, they roam the space-ways bringing profit to themselves and trade goods

to the twenty-five thousand odd settled worlds of the known galaxy. Not that the humans don't occupy planets - over eight thousand are recorded, but some dark remainder from Man's bleak and brooding past would seem to have caused each and every human world to fiercely maintain its independence, its history, its ideals, its religion, its feudalism and peasantry - and its poverty.

But strange to say some weird affinity would seem to link the Gods and the peasants, for Humanity, with its dark and evil past, and the Klylii who have never yet failed to breathe the essence of peace and goodness wherever they go, seem to have some kind of fatal attraction for each other: fully 80% of all recorded face-to-face confrontations with one or more Klylii individuals, have been with humans. With only one exception, all the known experts on the Klylii and their works have been human. That most such specialists have vanished mysteriously, their life work far from complete though giving thought for conjecture, can surely be little more than unfortunate coincidence; foolish accidents probably caused through the too keen following up of a more obscure clue as to the whereabouts of some hitherto unrecorded Klylii miracle.

But encounters between Humanity and the Klylii go back further than even the most optimistic and inventive of historians believe – back to the dawn of Human history in fact, thousands of years before the birth of Christ. But this story is concerned with the fist coming together of the two races during modern times, towards the end of the twentieth century in fact.

  The common was strangely quiet. In fact, Mark amended to himself having checked his watch, it was totally deserted. Strange. Normally at this time of the night, nine-thirty on a dry not-too-cold September evening, the place would have been, if not precisely crawling, at least respectably inhabited. But there wasn't a soul to be seen as far as the eye could range: no ambling pairs of lovers, no homeward bound late-night off-licence shoppers, no hurrying husbands with the latest hit video tucked under his arm, no conscientious dog-walkers deliberately avoiding all three of the village's public houses, no marauding bands of teenagers out for a spree.... Just nobody at all.
  Mark shrugged his shoulders philosophically - maybe there was something terrifically super on television, and maybe it was just a coincidence. He bent down to release the lead-clip from Susie's collar, and watched the gold coloured patch of racing Labrador streak away over the darkened grassy undulations. He carefully eased the lead into his coat pocket, turned up his collar against the expected gusting that would inevitably meet him as he reached the end of the hedge, and strolled slowly in the wake of the gamboling young bitch.
  The dog had rejoined him - theoretically. At least she was snuffling around the roots of a struggling cotoneaster some eight or ten feet away from where he stood gazing upwards, failing to identify most of the stars over his head when suddenly a small section of the heavens disappeared: a section which rapidly grew larger and larger. A faint whistling noise became audible, and it rapidly came apparent to Mark

that some kind of aircraft was flying extremely low over a built-up area of land. His first thought was annoyance at the deliberate flouting of regulations by some young idiot of an air-force pilot - on tax-payer's money, his money! His next thought was that possibly he and Susie were about to become the centre of the biggest air-disaster since Lockerbie, and he looked swiftly around at the almost invisible ring of orange street-lights, wondering what was the best direction in which to run.

His third thought was that surely any normal aircraft would be making much more noise and should be showing at least port and starboard navigation lights. However before more than half a dozen wilder flights of fancy had time to race through his mind (drug smugglers, illegal immigrants, D-Day paratroopers emerging from a time-warp) the descending object settled itself down on the ground about a hundred and fifty feet away directly in front of him. Susie's hackles rose, and she growled deep in her throat, sinking down at the front end. Mark swallowed convulsively and automatically started to ease the lead out of his pocket. His eyes were fixed on the apparition in front of him. It could be described in any of a score of ways, but that which sprang most readily to mind was that of 'saucer'. A flying saucer! It looked to be about sixty or seventy feet in diameter, and some fifteen thick at its widest or middle section. It stood perfectly silently on three short stout legs as Mark slowly approached, with a reluctant (and noisy) Susie pacing him.

All at once a faint noise came from the darkened object, and just silhouetted against the distant sodium lamps Mark saw something descending from the underside. It was rather like a ramp lowering itself to the ground, and from the hole thus created in the belly of the craft above, a faint whitish light shone down. The light was briefly occluded, and then he saw a shadowy human-like form descending the ramp. Susie gave a brief high pitched yelp and took off like an express train away across the grass in the opposite direction from the descending biped - roughly homewards. Mark barely noticed her going, being too taken up by twin intriguing thoughts: just who and what had he encountered and, why was he himself not sprinting in a terrified fashion for his life also.

The creature had reached the bottom of its ramp, but had moved forwards so that the available illumination merely served to show a black outline. Mark kept slowly advancing and the figure came equally unhurriedly towards him. They stopped, some ten feet apart with the visitor just clear of the overhang of the landed 'saucer' and Mark was able to make out some details: it was a woman - an extremely tall woman, well over six feet. That much was perfectly obvious for, apart from some kind of very brief skirt, she was completely naked! Not a terribly practical outfit for a September evening in the north of England. He took a step closer and cleared his throat.

"Good evening. Can I be of any.... um.... any.... er assistance?" Spoken out loud it sounded remarkably foolish to his ears, but having started he doggedly continued, "Looking for directions? Need water or something? Perhaps there's...." He trailed off into a foolish silence. Belated he realized that looking human didn't necessarily guarantee a knowledge of the English language as could be demonstrated any day of the week in a thousand different countries of the world. Beings who came whistling silently down out of thin air in strange ellipsoidal alien spaceships....

The being opened her mouth and laughed - a musical trilling sound that caused Mark's breath to catch in his throat. "Yes indeed you may Mark. Considerable assistance to me if you will." Her voice was like her laughter, light and musical - a sheer delight to hear

The man gasped, and swallowed convulsively. Having convinced himself that communications was likely to be a near insuperable barrier.... "Oh. Yes. Fine, of course I.... How did you know my name?" He belated queried. She shrugged and put her head on one side, staring enigmatically down at him. "You look rather like a 'Mark'. I just took a risk. It seems to have been worth it! Come." She extended her hand towards him, "I'll show you how you can be of immeasurable service to me and my people, The Klylii. Just a very few short hours of your time is all I ask."

Numbly Mark took the proffered hand. It was cold, yet seemed warm. Susie would have reached the house by now, he thought inconsequentially. She would have been barking at the back gate. Janet would let her in, and instantly go into utter panic over his absence. Perhaps she was even now struggling into her coat, warning the children not to answer either door or telephone. Or perhaps she was phoning the police, or knocking at a neighbour's door. He could hear the worried talk, the hunting out of torches, looking for Susie's old lead - the search party spreading itself out to scour the entire common.... Irresistibly he let himself be walked under the spreading crouching presence of the vessel, up the sloping ramp into the warm brightly lit interior of a visiting space-ship, his wife, family and home seeming unimportant irrelevancies beside the warm/cold pressure of the long alien fingers tucked securely in his.

THE spaceship waited in orbit. A vast creation that grew bigger and bigger and bigger to finally overwhelm his every concept of scale completely - what he had at first though of as being a tiny porthole instead turning out to be a gaping entry-port through which the saucer-shaped landing craft flew effortlessly with room for another ten on either side to accompany it. He blinked and shook his head in amazed bewilderment. It had to be many, many miles in length - ten, twenty, possibly even as much as fifty miles from stem to stern. Now that WAS a spaceship in anyone's book - made the American's vaunted shuttle look like a second-hand housefly. He wondered briefly why every alarm bell and early warning device in two hemispheres weren't sounding off hysterically, Perhaps they were he concluded cynically, maybe that explained the paucity of the park's population, and maybe it was just a coincidence, for surely a people capable of putting the equivalent of a London-sized city into outer space would be able to deal with something as crude and mundane as radar.

The saucer settled down inside its hanger, the great shutters slid closed overhead, and within an amazingly short space of time he was walking down the ramp into the vast echoing interior. It was a good hundred yards high and twice, three times that in length and breadth, containing a handful of other, identical machines together with an assorted collection of other larger craft of radically different design - built instead on the lines of the great parent ship which were roughly cylindrical with triple legs emerging from either end.

Mark, contemplating the nearest wall, the width of a football pitch distant, wondered briefly how one got from one part of the spaceship to another. He soon found out, and after two hours steady marching along seemingly endless corridors, seeing nothing and no-one other than his single companion was starting to wonder if perhaps it was help over the design of some form of railway that they needed him for.

He tried making polite conversation with his guide, commenting on the size of the great ship, but elicited very little real information other than a few basics about the race which called themselves 'The Klylii'. They apparently originated from the planet Klyl which circled a blue giant star some considerable distance away: she was vague about actual distances, but it seemed that it was several thousand light years distant, and although she admitted that the average Klylii tended to live longer than human beings (by how much she would not commit herself), it was clear that Klylii designed spacecraft were not limited by the speed of light. Mark exclaimed at this, "I always KNEW there was something aesthetically wrong about Relativity Theory" and allowed himself to be diverted into a semi-technical discussion from which he derived great personal satisfaction, but learned absolutely nothing of any practical value, or indeed of interest as regards The Klylii's manners, morals, and general habits - as had been his companion's intent from the start.

An hour passed reasonably pleasantly in this fashion but after a second more silent one had gone by and Mark, visibly flagging, was beginning to wonder if they were doomed to keep on walking for ever, Denella (which was how his guide had introduced herself) turned abruptly to the right under a vaulted archway. Half comatose he walked straight on, until called back. "Mark! Through here please." He stopped, turned and slowly came back in under the arch. "You must be tired and weary." She said. "Please rest yourself for as long as you wish. In the.... morning, I will return, and then with you refreshed, it will be soon enough to.... er.... discuss business." She abruptly exited. Mark called after her, but there was no response. He looked curiously about him. He was standing in a large beautiful room. Above stretched a domed ceiling, tastefully decorated in a pastel blue shade which met at an elaborate cornice, a continuous elliptical wall - decorated in a slightly darker shade of blue - which was broken by two graceful archways, just inside one of which Mark stood. Each arch occupied the centre of each of the shallower curves. There was a magnificent bed that fitted into one of the sharper curves - it was surrounded by three shallow steps - and opposite it sat a long low table beneath an elliptical mirror. The bed itself was oval and about three yards long. It occupied perhaps a fifth of the floor area.

The floor was soft, warm and resilient, like the better quality of carpeting. The table top carried a number of minor items - mundane in their normality such as a hair brush, comb and so on, but the table itself seemed to have been made from a solid block of marble.

Mark advanced further into the room, slowly turning round before approaching the mirror. Amidst such simplicity, it was hard to realise that the mirror was a miracle of optics. Perfectly flat and vertical, two feet by one, it hung at face level, yet reflected his complete figure without distortion, from a distance of less than three feet. Shaking his head, the man wandered off towards the other archway. It was more of a short passageway piercing a wall that was about twelve feet thick, and he could hardly keep back a gasp of amazement as he saw what lay at the end of it. It was a bathroom, in that it contained a bath - or more properly a pool - the green water rippling invitingly from its twenty by thirty yard elliptical expanse. The pool was ringed by a three yard wide ledge made out of the same marble as the bedroom dressing table, as were the walls and domed ceiling. The 'bathroom' was evenly and clearly lit, as was the bedroom, but no light source was in evidence.

He walked forwards towards a set of curved steps which ran from the pool's edge down in to the water, and noticed behind him and to either side a pair of deep arched recesses. One contained a set of what looked like eight shower heads. The other contained a set of strangely familiar items which made him think that Denella and her people regarded personal privacy as a state of mind rather than a matter of locked doors. Seeing everything displayed was father to the urge, and he discovered the facilities simple in the extreme to operate. The equipment also included brush, comb and so on, and he leisurely put them to use before going to examine the far opening. As he crossed over the threshold, he was instantly drowned in a deluge of water as every shower head burst into torrential activity.

Cursing and spluttering he backed out, noting with a tiny portion of his mind that the water had cut itself off just as quickly. He stripped off his wet clothes, leaving them in a soggy heap by the pool-side. About to go in search of something, anything to take their place, he was beguiled by the sparkling attraction of the pool and, without too much reluctance, succumbed, spending the better part of half an hour recapturing something of his lost youth as he cavorted around in emulation of a playful dolphin.

Finally he climbed out, and dripping water everywhere (though amazingly enough apparently wetting nothing!) he went off in search of towels and/or something to do duty as a bathrobe. He found neither, but as the search extended itself so did his body dry naturally. Discovering this, he abandoned the idea of a towel and, having glanced once at his dangling hairiness in the mirror, concentrated on something, anything, to conceal his nudity - sheer habit of course, but the idea that at any instant numberless statuesque green skinned Amazons with amber eyes and amber hair (that seemed to grow around the waist as well as on the head) could come waltzing in on him was one that it was difficult to forget.

The last place he thought to look was, of course, the dressing-table drawers. There were twelve of them in a double row of six. He slid one out, feeling its weight and instantly realised that whatever they were constructed from, it was not real marble. Inside the drawer lay several pieces of folded fabric, the top one of which, shaken out, revealed itself to be a garment - a skirt. It was short, off white in colour patterned with a delicate faint tracery of gold, and its texture was like that of silk, only with a wool-like warmth of feel to it. It seemed to be made all in one piece, yet had the feel of a woven textile. There was no hem at either top or bottom, but there was a thickening, that suggested a waistband, and a similar slimmer arrangement at the opposite end. He carefully laid it down across the table top and investigated further, lifting out the item below. It was another skirt - identical to its predecessor. There were three other identical garments in the drawer, and five more in each of the other eleven. There was nothing else. Mark sighed, closing the last drawer regretfully and picked up the garment he'd left draped over the table top. If that was all there was....

He stepped gingerly into it and pulled it up. It fitted snugly around his hips, as if made to measure, seeming to cling lightly, but without pressure of any kind. The hem terminated some ten inches above the knee, rather like the more extreme mini-skirts which his sisters had been forbidden to wear back in the nineteen-sixties. He twisted round, observing his rear in the mirror - it did, just conceal his buttocks, but it was a very close run thing.... He shrugged, discovered that the waistband was not susceptible to downward tugs and went off to see if there was anywhere that might double as some kind of drying rack for his own clothes.

A second extensive search failed to reveal anything of the kind. It also brought to light the intriguing fact that the search was somewhat pointless, some kindly agency having tidily removed the sopping bundle from the pool's edge.

Mark gazed down at the place where could have sworn he'd dumped them. Perhaps some obliging soul was even now stuffing them into the alien equivalent of a tumble-drier he thought cynically to himself, on the other hand.... It was probably a ten-to-one chance that he'd never see them again.

"Ah well," he sighed philosophically to himself, unaware that he was speaking out loud, "Let's make the best of things. Pretend it's great-grandfather MacDonald's kilt." He yawned, looked at the place on his wrist where his watch should have been, and sighed again. Luckily it had been an inexpensive item with no significant emotional attachments. Nine-thirty when he'd left the house with Susie. Must be well after midnight, nearer one, possibly two. No wonder he was tired. He headed for the vast bed, discarding his recently acquired garment on the second step, and snuggled gratefully down into the most comfortable berth he had ever encountered in his life.

Denella collected him some hours later, appearing as if by magic two minutes after he had completed his ablutions. She bowed politely, looking him expressionlessly up and down, making no mention of his change of apparel. Perhaps she had organised it. He had noted that the discarded 'kilt' had vanished from the bed-steps come morning and had been forced to raid the dressing-table drawers once more.

"If you would care to accompany me, there is a selection of food laid out for you to break your fast upon. It is not far to go."

Breakfast proved to be some kind of strange cereal vaguely reminiscent of oats together with a warmish drink that looked like coffee but tasted rather like orange juice. He ate alone in a pleasant apartment that seemed designed to act as both dining and sitting room for up to about half a dozen, and had just finished when Denella returned, accompanied by her twin sister. Except that it was actually two completely different beings. They introduced themselves.

"No, neither of us is D'nelaa. This is J'efti. I am J'asti." She paused, and indicated the small collection of low comfortable looking chairs which surrounded a small round table over on the far side of the room. "Perhaps things would be more comfortable if we sat down."

Mark nodded, not quite sure as to the exact significance of that final sentence. Was it a small mis-translation? Or not. He waited politely for the two ladies to seat themselves, then belatedly realising that J'asti's gesturing arm was to be taken literally, finally crossed over and carefully disposed himself in the nearest easy chair. It was a tricky business this, sitting down in a soft reclining seat whilst wearing the shortest of skirts. Was one supposed to flick the back up, or smooth it down. In the end it was something of an academic question, the bending of his body lifting the brief garment virtually out of contact with the seat. He leant back gradually, and discovered the advantages of keeping ones knee's firmly pressed together. It was slightly more comfortable to let them incline somewhat to the side, so he did that, relieved to discover that neither of his hostesses had picked the chair opposite him, preferring instead to sit one upon either side.

There was a pause which developed into a silence, threatening to become an uncomfortable hiatus. Mark coughed and cleared his throat. He was starting to feel ever so slightly uncomfortable. "Er.... Denella said that you had a.... a task which you wanted me to perform."

"Yes." The one on the right - J'asti? They had got themselves sort of mixed up as the three had seated themselves, and he was unsure as to which was which. "There IS such a service which could you but perform, would put us eternally in your debt. It is not a difficult or dangerous chore but is one that unfortunately neither myself nor indeed any of us Klylii can perform."

"I see," said Mark blankly, not seeing at all, and patiently awaited further enlightenment. The left hand one spoke up, producing, presumably from beside her chair, a large sheet of what looked like strong white card. She handed it across to Mark.

"This is a depiction of a certain.... machine, or apparatus currently malfunctioning in this, our spaceship. It requires to be de-activated - fairly quickly for the malfunction hourly grows worse. Due to the nature of the fault, none of us can approach it to switch it off for it emits a particular frequency of.... sound to which our race is particularly sensitive and which pains us so severely that even now, none can approach nearer than about two of your miles. In an hour, that will have become three miles, and then five, then ten, until at a time not too far distant, the entire ship will be wholly uninhabitable."

"Oh!" Mark stared intently at the card balanced insecurely on his lap. It was in full colour and showed an immensely complex gadget that looked rather like a cross between Stevenson's 'Rocket', an early mainframe computer, and a large dish of blue spaghetti. There was no indication as the size of the thing, nor was the 'off' switch marked. He rather diffidently pointed out these inadequacies to his companions

"The overall height is some eighteen feet - about three times your own length. To activate it requires the removal of an access hatch which lies to the rear of the elevation actually displayed. You will approach it from the front, go round to the back and there, in the middle, and somewhat below eye level is a square cover standing slightly proud of the surrounding plating. It is about fifteen inches on a side. Around the perimeter are a number of faint round marks, each somewhat smaller than a human finger-nail - three to each side. This tool," J'efti handed over a dark red-handled object that resembled a screwdriver with a small metal tetrahedron stuck to the end of the blade, "Held above each such mark for two seconds or more whilst pressure is maintained on the handle, will cause the attachments to release, and with the last such, the cover will become free and can be easily pulled clear. In the opening so revealed will be seen three pairs of large screw terminals, one above the other, linked together by metal plates. The middle two terminals must be unscrewed and the link plate removed. Then the top pair must be similarly dealt with. Once both link plates have been completely removed, they must be replaced at right angles, one plate joining the right hand pair, the other linking the left hand two - in that order, the first pair of terminals being screwed tightly up before proceeding to the second. Once the new links are secure and tight, THEN, and only then must the bottom link be removed - that final action will de-activate the mechanism completely."

"I see. It all seems fairly straightforward. Although I can't help thinking that an on-off switch would be a whole lot quicker and simpler."

"That would indeed be the case. Unfortunately when it was built - about four hundred of your years ago - its designer did not foresee any need to switch it off and on at regular intervals. I fear that we have been guilty of falling into the trap of believing that a construct which had performed faultlessly for such a period would continue to do so indefinitely, and had possibly allowed our preventative maintenance programme to suffer accordingly."

"Oh." Mark felt suitably chastened. The very idea of a complex machine operating continuously from the reign of Elizabeth the First all the way through to that of Elizabeth the Second - through fifteen generations of his family - was mind-boggling to say the least. An on-off switch certainly WOULD be an expensive luxury in such a case. He tried to think of anything created by his own race that could compare, and failed miserably. The nearest approach would be some sort of woodworm-riddled one-handed long-case clock that required winding weekly and would probably have had all its brass gears replaced several times over during the intervening centuries. He scrutinised the picture closely, endeavouring to imprint its salient features on his memory. "Whereabouts is this machine? When do you want me to do the job?"

J'efti (or J'asti) stood up. "The sooner the better. If you feel suitably refreshed, you might as well start now."

"Start? Refreshed?" Mark frowned and looked from one to the other. "Surely the task isn't going to take longer than five minutes or so?"

"That is substantially correct, but unfortunately you have to get there first, and I'm afraid this is rather a large vessel. A three hour walk is about what will be required to get you there. We will guide you part of the way, but can only get so near, and you must make your own way over the latter portions. We will give you clear directions of course."

Mark nodded. Three hours to get there implied three hours for the return hike. He shrugged philosophically. "Ah well. Better make a start then I suppose. Lead on."

Even after the first hour it was noticeable that the two Klylii were suffering. They were walking more slowly and their speech was becoming noticeably slower than before, with longish pauses between remarks. By the hour and a half stage they were virtually staggering, holding each other upright. Mark stopped.

"This is crazy. You'd better go back whilst you can. I've got the diagram and it all looks wholly straightforward from here."

"You're quite sure?" Whispered J'asti (or J'efti)

"Yes. I'll be fine. Go back while you can. Didn't you say that it was gradually increasing?"

"Very well. We thank you. Please be careful." They hobbled off, slowly making their way back along the high wide corridor which seemed to stretch endlessly in both directions. Mark waited, watching their progress and, before their figures diminished into insignificance by distance, noticed that they seemed to be moving more easily. He started walking again himself in the opposite direction just before they vanished out of sight - it would be so easy to loose all sense of direction and start going the wrong way. He consulted the small piece of card, screwing his eyes up to peer into the distance ahead. Was that the end of the corridor in sight?

His directions, though complex were clear and unambiguous, and another hour found Mark slowly traversing a long spidery openwork metal catwalk that crossed the immensity of a huge chamber containing the most incredible assortment of 'things' imaginable. He presumed it must be something analogous to the engine room - there was a certain similarity between his surroundings and those encountered many years ago when, as a young child on holiday, he had been thrilled to have been allowed to visit the engine rooms on one of the long vanished small pleasure steamships that used to cruise along the river Clyde from Glasgow to the Argyllshire coast: a sort of stark simplicity of purpose with no concessions made.

He reached a fancy multi-way junction and consulted his card. Half left, and then a long dead straight run before a right turn which should finally bring the rogue machine in sight, and so it proved; distant, but unmistakable. Involuntarily his pace quickened with his destination in sight. The result was foreseeable and within a very short space of time one foot caught in the lattice-work and he sprawled helplessly on his face, arms flailing wildly, unable to arrest his fall, or even cushion it. He lay half winded, watching the white card see-sawing into the endless void beneath, gradually growing smaller and smaller with distance until it was obscured by the intervention of some alien artifact.

"Oh shit!" He briefly closed his eyes. "Let's hope I can remember how to get back the way I came" He drew himself awkwardly on to his hands and knees, examining his palms and arms one by one: a few grazes but nothing serious. He reached up to grasp a convenient stanchion, and started to haul himself to his feet - only to stop as an agonising pain lanced through his left ankle. He closed his eyes briefly, the sweat springing out on his forehead and he gasped audibly with the effort of holding back an involuntary yell. "Oh brilliant Richards. Absolutely terrific! So you've just broken your bloody ankle. Now what? Lie here till you rot? Remember: none of the Klylii can make it this far themselves!"

He struggled to turn over until in a sitting position and gingerly felt round the affected member, pressing and squeezing gently. He tried to remember what little first aid he had learned, way back in the dim and distant past of his teen years, before the attractions of the cafe on the corner had proved superior to the long-windedness of the St John's Ambulance lady - kind but dull. Perhaps it was only twisted or strained, not broken after all. With a struggle, he managed to pull himself approximately vertical, and applied a small amount of load to his left leg. Not too bad. He leant rather more heavily, and tried to take a step forward: painful, but just possible with the support of the handrail.

Slowly he edged nearer his goal, painfully inching his way along the catwalk until, after nearly an hour's agonising shuffling, he was within a dozen yards of the offending gadget - and met a slight snag. It stood in splendid isolation where four catwalks met a massive cross-brace that carried a wide spiral staircase, and something that might have been a lift-shaft. To accommodate such an important junction, the ship's designers had created a broad landing: a great wide circular area, some twenty-five yards in diameter that was wholly innocent of handrails or supports of any kind. Mark took a deep breath, cautiously lowered himself to the cold lattice work under his feet, and started crawling doggedly forward. Half way across a metallic rattling noise arrested his progress, and he was just in time to stop the red handled screwdriver from vanishing into oblivion through a larger than normal slot in the metal-work. Clearly the unusual horizontal movements of his body had caused the instrument to work its way free from the waistband of his skirt. He broke out in a cold sweat, and remained frozen for a full five minutes, his hand gripping the little tool so tightly that his knuckles gleamed white and painful. Slowly he relaxed, blinking slightly. What was he DOING here? Why was he getting so worked up over what was really none of his business? Why hadn't he just turned round, declared himself physically unfit, and asked them to find themselves another sucker

A small voice inside told him it was a matter of respect - self respect, and giving a helping hand to other beings in distress. He'd had his chance, way back on the common to tell Denella to go chase herself. It was too late to back out now that a few odd difficulties had popped out of the woodwork. Mark had never held a terribly high opinion of his own moral standards, but reneging on a deal was something he abhorred in others and had always done his utmost to avoid perpetrating himself.

He briefly considered ways of safeguarding the vital instrument over the last few feet of his journey. His present scanty attire might be all that was required aboard the Klylii space-craft with its constantly maintained seventy-eight degrees, but there was no denying that a pair of stout jeans carried a useful assortment of pockets, and even the cheapest pair of shoes would probably have prevented his tumble. "Ah well," he sighed. It seemed there was nothing else for it and, feeling like an extra from *'Sinbad and the Pirates of the Seven Seas'*, recommenced his journey, the red handled screwdriver clenched firmly between his teeth. After a very short interval, he was convinced that the buccaneers of yore either travelled very swiftly over extremely short distances, or else had possessed specially designed jaws. It was agony!

Finally he reached the towering complexity that was the faulty machine. He looked up at it, removing the tool from his mouth, and awkwardly hauled himself upright once more, using some conveniently placed projections on the thing itself. He worked his way round to the back, carefully laid the screwdriver in a handy secure channel at waist level, and set about regaining his breath, and something of his equilibrium.

He closed his eyes, clinging on to the machine for dear life as a sudden upswell of nausea washed over him. He shuddered, only just prevented himself from losing his last meal, and waited whilst the feeling subsided. He shook his head, blinking and took a deep breath. That's what came of getting up too quickly he thought, and looked around for the square plate.

'But it's been over thirty asts since we left it in the long corridor. The human should have deactivated the aerinsilith modulator at least ten, more likely fifteen asts ago. It had little more than twelve lamadns to cover, no more than an hour of its time at a steady walk.' J'sfti (in the physical person of J'asti) paced restlessly along the broad sweep of the main bridge instrumentation. H'llayr gave the mental equivalent of a shrug.

'Perhaps it got lost, or distracted along the way. From what you've told me you didn't exactly claim extreme urgency for the project.'

'Of course not. There was ample time - then. But who could have predicted such a discontinuous shift in the amplitude-restrictor decay mechanism. In another forty asts this very bridge will become uninhabitable: in twenty the uncontrolled emanations will start to affect the mentation of the human being making de-activation virtually impossible - even now there will be very faint effects noticeable to it. And that's quite apart from the electro-mechanical and particular disturbances - neutron bombardment and gamma radiation the humans call it. They can have quite a long term disruptive effect on the more delicate animate tissues of certain beings. I wish I'd studied the inner workings of the human more closely whilst I'd the chance. I'm getting rather worried about its medium to long term safety.'

'So I should think. And if it doesn't kill the machine soon it'll be the poor creature's short term safety we'll be concerned about. We can probably get clear in one or more of the small auxiliaries, but no power available to us here and now can get the human away from where ever it's got itself to. You will recall D'nelaa calculated that it would take some five masts to modify a robot sufficiently to give it an even chance of survival, which was why it was decided to obtain a volunteer from the nearest indigenous populace.'

'I would hardly describe what D'nelaa did to get the human up here a case of "volunteering" - given half a chance to use its own mind and reactions naturally, it would have been off away after its smaller four-footed companion long before she'd even reached the foot of the ramp. Not an episode to be particularly proud of I fear - the ethics in the case falling sadly below our usual standard.'

'We could hardly have been expected to anticipate all the strange and unexpected delays that seem to have crept in to the schedule. It should have disabled the modulator long since - what CAN be keeping it?'

'I don't know H'llayr,' J'asti took another turn along the long sweep of instrumentation, *'The whole thing just seems to be running wildly out of control.'* She stood over the section of the board which would first show up declining activity by the faulty modulator, almost as if She were willing the displays to change for the better.

The attack of nausea finally passed away - at least, sufficiently so for Mark to contemplate starting the job he had come to perform. He picked up the red-handled tool and steadied himself by tightly gripping what looked rather like a brass stand-pipe. He carefully scrutinised the flat section of machine around eye-level and almost at once found the square plate referred to. It was right in the middle, and just out of reach from where he stood. He eyed up the far side. Was the whole thing completely symmetrical? It seemed from where he hung that perhaps the far away pipe might just be somewhat nearer the plate. Two feet would be enough. He replaced the tool in his mouth and carefully eased himself back down on to his hands and knees once more.

It WAS slightly nearer, just near enough to allow him at full stretch to apply the tool to the far edge of the plate. Unfortunately he couldn't quite see what he was doing and had to rely on guess and luck. A faint 'tic' was the only indication that he had hit the mark, and that only after the tool had done its silent work. The most distant side he had figured would be the worst and so had tackled it first. For some reason though, possibly continuing fatigue in his outstretched arm, it was the nearer fastenings which were proving most recalcitrant. Time and time he tried, holding his breath for an incredibly long two full seconds, and time and again his shoulders slumped before he forced himself to try yet again. At last he hit one on the mark, then, three tries later the next. But it was a full five minutes of sweated agony before the final one yielded. Slowly, almost gracefully the released plate slid down to the decking. Mark didn't even see it. He was hugging his supportive pipe, eyes closed, as another bout of wretched nausea washed over his shivering frame. This second attack passed off more swiftly, but left him feeling rather odd. Nothing he could put a finger on, but....

He straightened up, glancing sideways, and instantly noted the difference: a square cavity was now revealed. He stretched out a strangely heavy arm and discovered there was a lip running all the way round. The sweat stood out on his forehead in relief - something to hang on to close at hand! He replaced the screwdriver in his sadly abused mouth, carefully worked his way sideways and, gripping the sides with both hands, peered into the recess he had finally managed to reveal. The sets of terminals and their link rods were plainly in view - bigger than he had expected. He squinted downwards and sideways. The machine's outer casing appeared to be just that: there was no convenient ledge inside the opening in which to lay down the screwdriver or to provide a temporary resting place for the terminals. He carefully lowered himself to the ground. Was it imagination, or was his ankle hurting rather less than it had to begin with - it was hard to say. Certainly the sudden stabbing twinges occasioned by incautious movements seemed less severe, but the overall throbbing pain that embraced his entire leg, foot and whatever, was probably worse.

Mark resolutely tried to ignore the aching that was spreading insidiously through his body and laid the detached inspection cover-plate flat on the metal decking to provide somewhere to place any bits and pieces. He started to struggle to his feet once more, looked critically at the plate, and then moved it a yard away. Better a bit of inconvenience than to risk kicking something off it into the vast emptiness below. He struggled upright, gripping on to the edge of the opening, and examined the interior once more. He had written down the detailed instructions on the directions card, but that was fled to goodness knows where. Middle followed by top link removed, and then.... and then.... He cudgelled his brain, striving to remember. Was it Right then left, or left then right? The more he tried, the less certain he became. "Oh well!" He shrugged, speaking aloud to the echoing loneliness around him, "Let's get the first bit done first. Maybe it'll come back in time." He gripped the left hand terminal of the middle pair between thumb and forefinger and twisted. Nothing happened. He gripped the knurled metal knob somewhat tighter and applied more pressure. Still no result. He swore gently under his breath and tried the right hand one with equal lack of success. He re-applied himself to the left hand one once more, and re-adjusted his stance and grip in order to provide slightly greater purchase on the offending objects, and tried once more.

Ten minutes of struggling, tugging, swaying and blaspheming saw him no further forward. He had lost his grip twice, fallen once, and suffered yet another attack of nausea. He was starting to get desperate, his breath becoming laboured, the sweat running down his face and body, no part of which seemed free from some kind of hurt or other. He pushed his soaking wet hair out of his eyes and tried to calm down, to think.

Why had the Klylii not provided him with some kind of spanner, pliers or some other sort of tool with which to grip the recalcitrant terminals? Presumably because they considered them to be easily unscrewable by hand - yet from what had been told him, it seemed likely that no one had even looked at them for four hundred years or so. Surely the possibility of corrosion, diffusion or something of the like should have presented itself. He gripped the edge tightly with both hands, hauled himself up on to his one good tip-toe and thrust his head as far into the opening as possible, examining the lowest terminal as closely as he could. It seemed perfectly standard, a short length of screwed rod about a quarter of an inch in diameter with a knurled knob about an inch and a half wide threaded upon it. There was a tiny section of rod protruding through and on it he could see.... he could see the threads. A sudden thought, staggering in its simplicity, struck him and almost tentatively he pulled back and reached out a hand towards the terminal he had been examining, changed his mind and grasped the left-handed centre one. Slowly he twisted clockwise, the direction which a life-time's instinct insisted would TIGHTEN up the nut. Slowly it rotated, gradually winding itself outwards along the threaded shaft. Mark took a deep breath, and slowly counted up to twenty - using binary notation. Carefully he transferred the first knob to the waiting plate, then the second one to be shortly joined by the piece of shining flat metal that had linked the two terminals together. Quickly the second set of knobs joined them. He held the top link plate in his hand and was about to start re linking the studs vertically when the by now familiar nausea hit him - a long and severe dose. He collapsed to his knees, so severe the cramps that he barely noticed the lancing agony that shot through his maltreated ankle in the process. He grasped the link plate tightly in convulsive reaction, the sharp metal digging unnoticed but deeply into the flesh of his hand.

Twenty miles away, on the bridge of the vast star-ship, a growing group of Klylii watched the displays changing with painful slowness.

'What IS the human doing to take so long,' H'llayr put first level substance to all their inner cogitations, 'Is it injured or something? The emanations surely cannot be affecting the human mentation already, and the radio-active output is hardly sufficient to have caused any significant tissue damage yet.'

'Of course not.' J'sfti (physically present as J'asti) contemplated the displays a second time. 'From the length of time that the human took to reach its goal I would suspect that it sustained some kind of injury. Remember that it formerly wore semi-rigid protective coverings on its feet. It might not be used to walking any great distances without such protection, especially over the openwork trunking of the drive chamber. Perhaps it tripped and injured one of its legs. That would account for the delay in reaching the modulator. It might also have mislaid the list of directions which could have slowed it even further.'

'True,' G'pytlr conceded, 'But why still so slow?'

'The access panel is quite high up - if the human is experiencing difficulty walking, it may well be having problems maintaining itself erect over a prolonged period.'

'Of course.' H'llayr replied, 'One tends to forget the limitations imposed by a purely physical.... The card which carried directions. Did it not also explain the sequence of link removal and replacement?'

'Yes, but they had been dictated verbally before the card was provided. They are simple enough. Surely no being could forget....'

'Let us hope not. If the vertical links are made in the wrong order the electro-mechanical and nucleon output will be increased twenty-fold or more from that time until the lower junction is removed, and at its current performance speed, that might well have unfortunate side effects.'

There was a lengthy hiatus, broken finally by G'pytlr. 'Let us hope then that the.... what is it that it describes itself as?'

'Man is the word you're looking for, I believe.' Put in D'nelaa.

'Of course. Let us hope therefore that the man remembers its instructions properly, and does not take too long over their execution.'

The man was trying desperately to fight off the urgings of his body to regurgitate the entire contents of its stomach preparatory to curling up into a tight little ball, and the last thing on his mind was whether the left or right links should be put in position first. All he wanted to do was to get the wretched job finished - goodness knows how he'd let himself be talked into it in the first place - and then find somewhere warm and quiet and dark and peaceful.... Finally the cramping agonies subsided somewhat, and he hauled himself vertical once more, two screw fixings in his mouth, and the first metal link clasped in his right hand. The link was put in place, then first one and then the second knob twisted back down to tightly clamp it in place. He lowered himself slowly back on to his haunches once more and reached out for the second link and its fixings, and within a very short time he had the right hand pair securely joined together.

Mark took a deep breath, "Nearly finished," he muttered under his breath and changed his grip slightly before reaching for the first of the terminals on the last remaining horizontal strip. One, two complete turns of the right hand knob he managed, before he felt the all to familiar feelings erupting from the depths of his abdomen. It was worse than any of the others, and he sagged helplessly to the decking writhing and moaning, unconscious of the terribly high levels of deadly radiation sweeping through his body.

On the bridge, D'nelaa was the first to realise the significance of the changing signals:

'It's got them the wrong way round!' Her second level exclamation drew everyone's attention. J'sfti (both of her by then physically present) gravely confirmed the configuration.

'If it can remove the lower link within fifty lamuns - two of its minutes - then there is a faint possibility that all may yet be well.' She glanced briefly at the timer display atop the console section. Already one quarter of that time had remorselessly slipped past. Everyone waited, eyes glued to the changing symbols, not a single concept could be detected over the whole conversational level of the group Klylii consciousness, yet everyone was aware - almost like an involuntary Consensus.

The fifty lamuns slipped into sixty, seventy.... a hundred. After a full three asts had passed by with the damning displays having changed not one iota, J'sfti turned away. J'efti shifted to the further end of the great horseshoe, and started calling up the status of the great ship's auxiliary vessels, whilst her other half, J'asti slowly paced up and down, her 'quarter-deck' walk only just removed from the cluster of control room personnel still waiting and hoping.

'Any chance at all do you think?' D'nelaa directed a very low power query at G'pytlr.

'Of the human's long term survival, none. Oh it may walk and talk and think for a while to come, but essentially it's dead. As regards the modulator, well, I don't think

our revered leader is checking out the auxiliary craft status for fun, do you? I suspect that She thinks the human could well be dead in fact as well as in essence.'

'Oh. Very pretty indeed. We drag this poor native away from its world and all it knows, to do OUR dirty work for us. For some reason it fails, and we just take off, abandoning it to a painful and lingering death aboard a deserted alien spaceship lost in the middle of nowhere.'

'Well, put like that, I don't suppose it sounds very estimable, but there's nothing any of us can do, after all. It's impossible to get within twenty lamadns of the modulator now, and its getting worse - you can sense the growing disruption already here, where until recently there was none at all. I mean it's only a single creature after all - an animal, one that not only consumes vegetation to stay alive, but even eats other animals!'

'I daresay, though that's hardly the man's fault is it. It was conned, however it regards its own actions, WE know that the man Mark Richards was forced into doing US a favour - I forced him to come here, and it's going to die a horrible painful death as a direct result. WE will have murdered it!'

'Oh come on now D'nelaa. That's putting it rather strongly. Anyway, you can only MURDER a member of one's own species.'

'You're simply quibbling, you know precisely what....'

'Indeed yes. The whole situation is quite as abhorrent to me as anyone, and I can't help but feel that it's likely to have dire effects in many unexpected directions for a long time to come. Living with one's self after having been party to such deeds as must forever....' J'sfti, who had insinuated herself unnoticed into what was threatening to become a heated argument, suddenly broke off as a great mental shout emanated from H'llayr:

'The displays! The human's finally done it! The modulator's been powered down at last!'

Instantly, J'sfti shifted both Her physical selves into the depths of the drive chamber, materialising almost to within touching distance of the human being who had risked his all - and lost - in the service of an alien race. With the rogue machine finally de-activated, no longer was a part of the great ship a forbidden mystery to its crew. J'asti bent down over the still sprawled figure before her and swiftly appraised its condition.

Either the electro-magnetic and particular radiation had been more severe and prolonged than estimated, or else the human species was peculiarly sensitive and susceptible to its effects. Mark Richards, Englishman, had not long to go. The injured ankle and its effects on him were in a way a blessing, having rendered him unconscious at the moment of completion of his task. He would not stay that way for long though without help. J'asti stood up, briefly examined the machine in front of her and turned towards H'llayr who was only one of ten or more Klylii who had appeared, anxious to help in whatever way possible. Behind her back, the last terminal, only three-quarters home, slowly screwed itself tightly into place. 'Take it to the larger bio-laboratory now,' J'sfti commanded, J'asti gesturing towards the cramped supine figure sprawled over the metal decking, its skirt rucked up to expose one pink buttock. *'G'pytlr, I want you to run a complete series of tests. Get F'calaa and F'galaa to help you with the asymmetric determinant factors. I want a full Q Analysis within the mast - sooner if possible.'*

'A full Q Analysis? In a single mast..... Should we not rather, without delay.... the human's own physicians and surgeons, more experienced with the weaknesses and failings of their own kind must have remedies and cures to hand. If we were to take it back to its own world....'

'You really think so? Examine the creature for yourself, and remember what D'nelaa's opinions are as to the reasons and responsibilities in the case. This is OUR fault, OUR problem. Anyway, you cannot resuscitate a corpse - the human is clearly dying, well past the point of no return. I doubt if any power in the known universe can reverse the changes even now spreading throughout its body.'

G'pytlr thoughtfully appraised the still silent, barely breathing form before her. Her knowledge of human physiology was scanty, to say the least, but even she could recognise a complex organism that was rapidly failing in almost every important aspect of its operation.

'I have to agree - it IS dead in all but fact. So why the Q Analysis? I mean it's hardly likely to live long enough for the analysis to be even partially completed.'

'Which is why it's vital to move the creature NOW - to immediately get the human into the Demi-Cylan Chamber without any further delay so that we can commence the Arrestment Process.'

'The Arrestment Process? Do you think that will be effective? And surely it can only delay things.'

'Of course it can at best only put off the moment of total dissolution. We can only try and do our best - exactly what the human did for us. There is an idea.... One slim chance.... Anyway, get it moved to the laboratory now, and start right away The more time wasted here in useless speculation, the less there will be available to us later, after all the various tests and assessments are over and the full analysis is completed.'

'Very well. We'll start right away.'

'Excellent.' J'sfti drew into Herself, remaining wholly withdrawn for several asts before finally coming to a decision - the decision that had never really been in doubt. *'F'galaa?'*

Once she set about doing a job the details of which were clear to her, there were few to match G'pytlr for dedication, attention to detail, and sheer unadulterated drive. J'sfti knew that better than anyone: the resulting analysis would be complete and wholly accurate; nothing would have been missed, overlooked, left to chance, or misinterpreted.

Whilst the unconscious human, Mark Richards lay stretched out (in an artificially induced coma) in the Demi-Cylan Chamber that was the most prominent feature of the larger bio-laboratory, his nearly useless body still slowly rotting away about him, J'sfti had been spending many asts of unremitting concentration carefully going through the myriad of test results, the preliminary Q Analysis, and collating all the masses of interdependent figures. The task was made no easier for possessing two sets of independently controlled eyes, hands and so on. Indeed, sometimes it made things unnecessarily complicated. But all that notwithstanding, the end result was arrived at with what amounted to amazing speed. She calmly contemplated the results, the long many complex tables of figures, then summoned H'dasa.

'How is the human's physical condition?'

'Not too good. I doubt if it can survive for very much longer. Certainly no more than a mast, if that. I'm actually surprised that it's still with us.'

'That bad eh? Very well. I want you to give it the full cryogenic treatment.'

'Full? You mean.... as we did for.... for the body of.... of.... H"orlaa?'

'Exactly.'

'But why? Of what possible use can the decaying corpse of a....'

'We have an obligation, H'dasa. The human sacrificed its all in our service - a service into which it was tricked. There is no other word to fully describe the circumstances. We owe it to human to do our utmost to repay that debt, but more importantly we owe it to ourselves! Now I seem to recall H'jati doing some very interesting research into the inter-dependence of self-induced conceptualisation of the inner and middle consciousnesses not all that many lamasts ago.'

There was a brief pause whilst H'dasa considered all the implications of J'sfti's comment.'

'I see. You think that the cases are suitably similar to attempt to take things to the logical conclusion.'

'I merely point out the results of your own research.'

'But that was before Pairing, and....'

'You doubt the validity of the conclusions?'

'No. I stand by my results.'

'Good. So now, is the time to take the next few steps. We have the body of H'orlaa. Let us now attempt to roll back the frontiers of knowledge a bit further - and discharge an obligation.'

'Discharge..... You mean..... My goodness!'

'Precisely. However,' J'efti waved an arm at the small mountain of test results spread out before Her. 'This is only part of the story you know. I've spent a long time thoroughly probing the human's mind. It is of amply sufficient quality, in all significant aspects, I assure you. Had it been otherwise, it would not now even be alive - despite all obligations. Some duties supersede others you appreciate.'

'Despite the obligation?'

'Indeed yes. Remember H'dasa that the crew of this one ship is all we are, here and now. The massed millions of Klyl are far distant in both space and time - unreachable within several lamasts without this ship; and the ninety-six of us that currently crew it and our twelve children are MY responsibility. I HAVE to take every conceivable precaution. I assure you, I have done just that on this occasion, and so will I answer before The Ship Council, before Full Council, and even Consensus!'

H'dasa briefly drew in on herself, considering deeply the myriad implications of such a pronouncement, and felt a weight lift. *'Ah. Reassuring. Misgivings now dispersed.. Thank you.'*

'One chance in ten J'sfti! Is it fair to divert such a great proportion of the ship's energies, and those of its people into a project with such slim odds of success. H'dasa has shown me the results of all her latest researches and experiments. There would appear to be several somewhat dubious assumptions in the base theory. Have you even asked the human if it WANTS us try such a thing on it. It could well be total anathema to its philosophy, to its entire way of thought.' H'fajw, earnestly put forward the case to J'sfti.

J'sfti, carefully refraining from probing the underflow, replied with a bald affirmative. She waited briefly for a repost, or invitation for higher congress before continuing.

'It is a prime obligation - suppose it were to take ALL the ship's energies and every last effort of all ninety-six of us. And with all due respect, I do not really consider you are in a position to challenge H'dasa's postulates: She is our chief expert on such matters and if She is satisfied then so am I - and so should you be.' She paused briefly before changing tack. *'I have not asked the human, nor do I intend to ask it. It is, as you must be aware, in total suspension and will remain that way until just before it leaves its body - whatever the destination. To bring it into such a state as to enable rational thought and provide replies to serious questions would inflict such pains as no thinking being could ever justify. It's whole body is disintegrating, rotting away. Warming and inducing consciousness now is wholly out of the question. In any case it is entirely unnecessary, as well as being totally undesirable, even if possible. Humans, for historical reasons, are virtually incapable of saying exactly what they want, or mean: they live crippled under a weight of complex tribal taboos and obligations. They frequently say what they think the auditor wants to hear from them. They decline from accepting what they most desire from social politeness, expecting to be persuaded into grateful acceptance. They persuade themselves into wanting what others think is best, or what is convenient, or economical. I have probed the being's mind over long periods and am satisfied. I know its aspirations, longings, fears - better than it does itself.'*

H'fajw made no return. The code was the code, and it was not really part of her duties, Senior Ship Counsellor or not, to remind Their Leader of what precisely the letter of The Law stated. But they had been through many trying times together, and the idea of J'sfti, for whatever reason, defying one of the prime canons....

'Might I enquire whether you request on behalf of the entire Ship Council, or merely as its chief member?'

'I simply ask You, as one Klylii to another if You should not reconsider, and TRY and obtain conscious, willing permission in its own style and format, before subjecting the primitive to what, if it succeeds, must surely be one of the most incredibly traumatic events imaginable - of such magnitude as, I am convinced, that not even any of us can

fully comprehend.' She paused, before adding, almost as a throwaway, *'And I'm sure You wouldn't wish to go against the Code.'*

'The Code.... ah yes. You wouldn't, by any chance be attempting to remind me of my obligations would you H'fajw?'

'Me? Remind You of Your obligations? Have I ever done anything like that? Would I ever do anything like that, to You, of all people?'

'Silly question." For a long, long time J'sfti made no response whatsoever, until finally, *'However, you ARE right, curse you. Oh well. Better done sooner than later. Anyone special in mind? Or would you be happy for D'nelaa to do the questioning - she knows the human as well as anyone I suppose - apart from myself of course, and that....'*

'D'nelaa was who I would have suggested. Perhaps H'llayr could take care of the poor creature's sensory centres and so forth....'

'Whilst you monitor and I observe - all strictly as per tradition and as laid down in the venerable texts of The Law.'

It was a nightmare. It had to be - surely! He'd been out walking the dog when this flying saucer had landed, and an impossibly beautiful, all but naked alien woman had asked him to perform a small act of charity for her which involved....

He shivered, could sense that there was a bright light shining on his face, and curious sounds impinged upon his hearing. There was a far from pleasant smell floating around also, like a rubbish heap left too long in the sun.. He struggled to open his eyes, but they remained gummily and obstinately closed.

"Mark? Are you hearing me Mark? Are you awake? Can you understand me? Nod your head slightly if you can - don't try and open your eyes yet."

He nodded his head slightly. That voice! Like a choir of heavenly angels, telling him he was awake when he had been convinced she was a figment of partially digested cheese! He struggled to open his eyes again. The effort failed, but there was a perceptible increase in brightness. He made to rub his right hand across his eyes and found a strange lack of response - almost as if he had no arm available to carry out his brain's commands!

He transferred responsibility to the left upper limb with an identical response. He drew a deep breath and discovered that there seemed to be an absence of chest movement.... in fact he seemed unaware of ANY part of his body past his head! He could sense some sort of soft vague pressure on the back of his head, a dryness about the mouth, the air moving in and out of his nostrils, but nothing more. And what was, if anything even worse than these anomalies, was the fact that he could work up no concern over them whatsoever.

His eyelids slowly lifted on the third try. Strange, the light was nowhere nearly as bright as he'd expected. A vague round blob swam hazily in front of him. He blinked, somewhat slowly, and struggled to focus. Gradually the picture clarified. It was a head, a face, and it spoke:

"How are you Mark? How do you feel?"

He blinked again - slightly more quickly. Presumably the eyelids were getting themselves gradually unstuck. "Still dreaming I see. Voice like an angel, with a face and figure to match - Denella, lovely Denella. Would that the greater half of humanity were one quarter so good." The voice was cracked and rusty - a harsh whisper issuing through swollen and bleeding lips. Behind and to one side of the high table H'llayr and H'fajw held a swift interchange:

'Strange mix of fact and fantasy. I wonder if it knows who she is, or was its choice of names just a lucky guess.'

'I daresay D'nelaa will be able to enlighten us in due course. How does it hear itself?'

'As it used to sound.'

'Good.'

D'nelaa continued her gentle questioning: "Are you in any pain Mark? How do you feel?" It was important to get a two-way dialogue operating: irrespective of what the human might THINK, it had to physically express its desires in its OWN way, that is, by physical speech.

There was a pause after her queries. Clearly the man was making some effort to reply, "No pain. No hands, no feet, no arms no legs, no chest no back. No-thing!" The man giggled slightly. "A play on words - not, I fear very original though. Oh Denella, Denella! What have I done to myself now. Such a simple task, yet the man from the back side of wherever mucked it up didn't he?"

"Hush," D'nelaa soothed, whilst she worked slowly through his sub-surface though patterns, trying to decide how best to introduce the concepts to which they required an answer. The human rambled on:

"I really screwed up didn't I? Ruined my leg, lost the instructions, couldn't figure out which way to turn, then got the thingies back to front, and finally collapsed with the job not even finished. Oh Shirley, Shirley! No one screws it up like me, do they?" A strange uneven noise issued from the cracked infected lips. The observers commented on it.

'It's really getting fact and fiction mixed up now. I wonder who or what Shirley might be?'

'I sense some logic. Ah, it's a song. It's trying to sing.'

'A song?'

'Yes. Wait, I'm searching.... I get fragments.... A popular singer called Shirley was, it seems, famed for a very popular song telling the tale of some human who could never do anything right.'

'Interesting.'

'Yes. Who knows . Perhaps the human would find some puzzlement viewing the leisure pursuits of us Klylii.'

'Possibly. Aha, I see D'nelaa's finally working round to it - clever!'

"Mark, can you hear me."

"Oh I hear you Denella. I see you too my angel. This must be the final vision of the dying man. Everyone has to die sometime. I suppose, this means my time has come now."

"Oh no Mark. Only those that the gods love die young - surely you must remember that. The rest of us, we have to climb slowly level by level, we must progress slowly upwards learning and forgiving on each of a myriad of different planes of existence. Do your learned instructors in philosophy not teach you such things?"

"Re-incarnation is a crutch for the insecure, for those who refuse to stand by their mistakes, and would wish-think themselves into a second chance. Dead is dead: the true follow-on can only be through the family and breeding a better race - proof positive that humanity is doomed. Let me die now, in ignorance," The weak cracked voice rose half an octave, and took on a faintly wavering tone, dropping, if anything, in volume even further. "And how can man die better, than through facing fearful odds, for the ashes of his fathers and the temples of the gods. And if you find the odds are long each time you come to play, why that's the game, the way it goes, so smile each time you pay." The half-remembered, half-impromptu rhyme dissolved into a bout of coughing which lasted an inordinate amount of time, and left the patient much weaker than before. D'nelaa leant closer - not that she needed to be, but he seemed to expect it of her. "Great laugh if it was all true," he whispered up at her almost inaudibly, "Imagine coming back as a stick-insect or a crane-fly, just because one didn't believe in it...." He laughed, an almost silent convulsive shudder, that was more harmful to him, and even worse to observe than the coughing had been. D'nelaa brought her face even closer, until their heads were almost touching. This was it, there could never be a better time.

"And if it WERE true Mark, what WOULD you want to come back as. How would you like to come back as someone, say, like myself - a Klylii?"

The failing voice was virtually inaudible - fortunately nobody needed to hear it. "Tha.... that's a poor kind of joke to play on a dying man, to summon up such images of wondrous enchantment. As well ask what I'd do if I won a couple of million pounds on the pools."

It was enough. *'I think that's ample to satisfy the code. You agree H'llayr?'* H'fajw shot an aside at D'nelaa, *'Put it under again now D'nelaa - back into stasis as a matter of supreme urgency. We have all we need. And if you can provide some enjoyable soothing dreams until then, I'm sure the human would appreciate the relief from its confusion.'*

H'llayr agreed. *'Amply sufficient for all purposes. Now, the really tricky part starts. H'dasa was telling me that the actual transfer ideally should be spread over something like two complete masts - assuming that the process actually works at all of course. I can't say I really understood what She was trying to tell me. She says that one can separate the mind up into twelve distinct sections, each with nine-hundred and eighty sub-sections, cross linked by something she described as "super-nodes". That's a Klylii mind of course. A human one she thought was somewhat less complex - three sections with fewer sub-sections. But She didn't seem to think the differences were really material just so long as one was able to line up the various sections'*

'Hmm. Interesting. And what did she think was the likelihood of success.'

'She was very coy over that one, I have to admit. Not a straight "One chance in three" or anything as simple apparently. There was some kind of sliding scale that got better or worse at various points during the process. And the whole was, of course, dependent on the subject living long enough for everything to be completed properly. Seems that the human's extreme fragility means that everything will have to be carried through at twice the optimum speed: not a good omen. Still, there must be some kind of a chance, otherwise I don't suppose J'sfti would have countenanced the diversion of such a large amount of time, skills and resources.' They departed at last, leaving D'nelaa alone with her patient.

"I never play jokes, Mark, she breathed softly into his left ear. "Angels are very serious people - didn't you know that? And though we may not always mean exactly what you think we say, we DO mean something by what we say. You performed for me, for all of us, a service the true value of which you may never know, and in performing that service gave your all. Not something to be lightly dismissed, nor will it. Now it's time to sleep, to sleep.... to sleep.... sleep....", and Mark Richards, human being, slipped into his last sleep, a sleep enlivened by the most wondrous dreams imaginable.

Find out what happens to Mark next,
in 'NOVICE'

FRAGMENTS OF A TIME TO COME

Words and Pictures

by

Frang McHardy

The Downkeeper warned his subjects that he didn't frighten easily. They understood, and not a squeak was heard in protest.

Had Bauldovix realized the nature of his wife's "extra tuition" earlier, he probably would have loosened the ceiling.

Binary Bill suffered a moment of inner conflict, when faced with either social exclusion or certain irradiation.

The last dragonfly expired and the Warden's heart broke. A terrifying finality struck him.

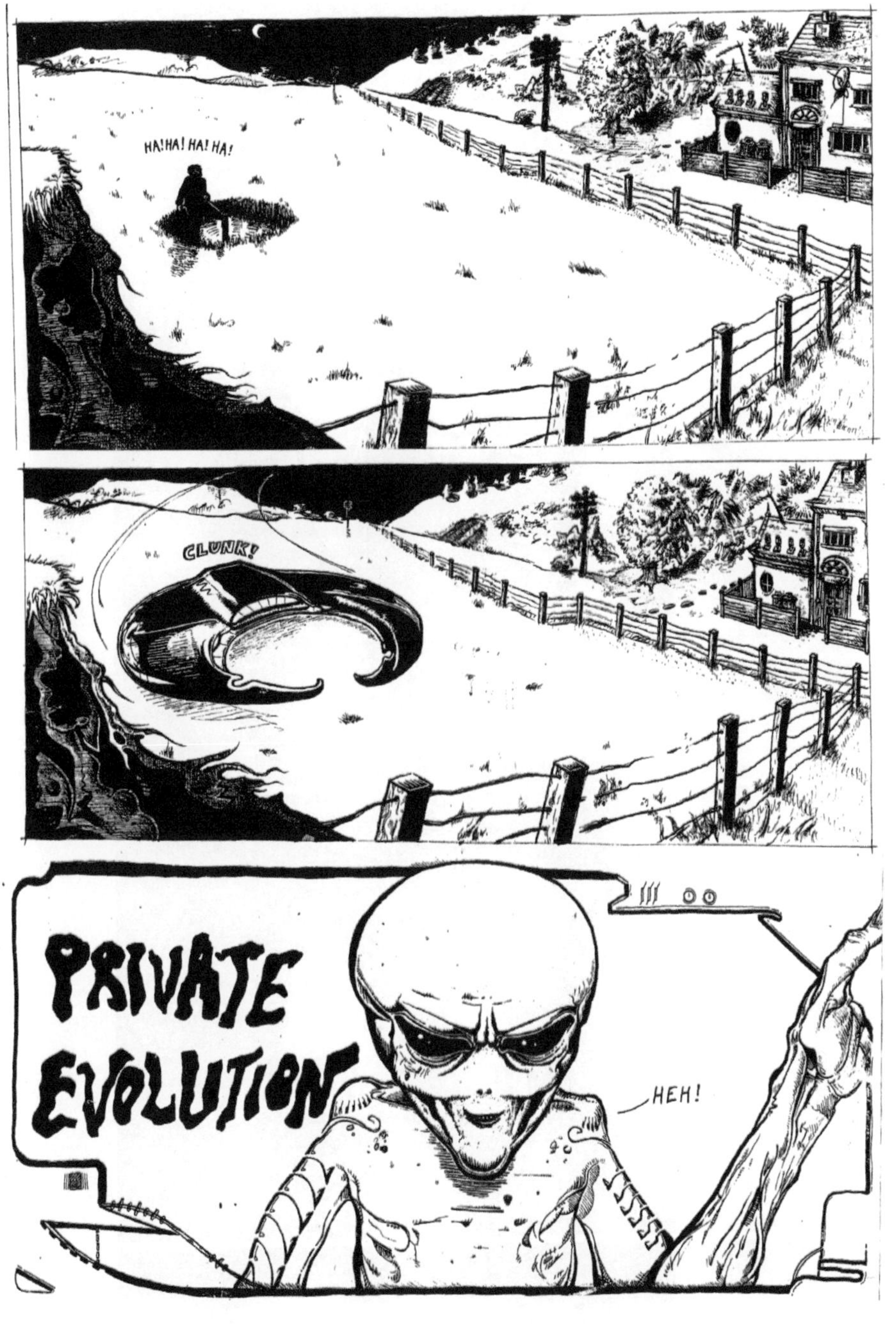

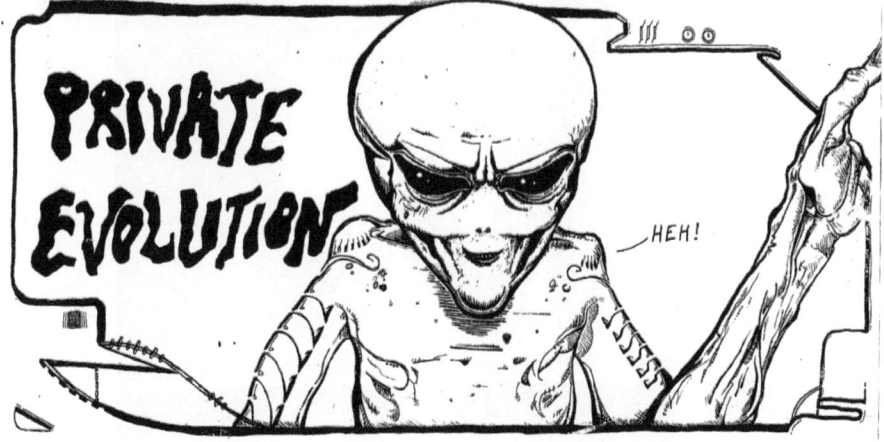

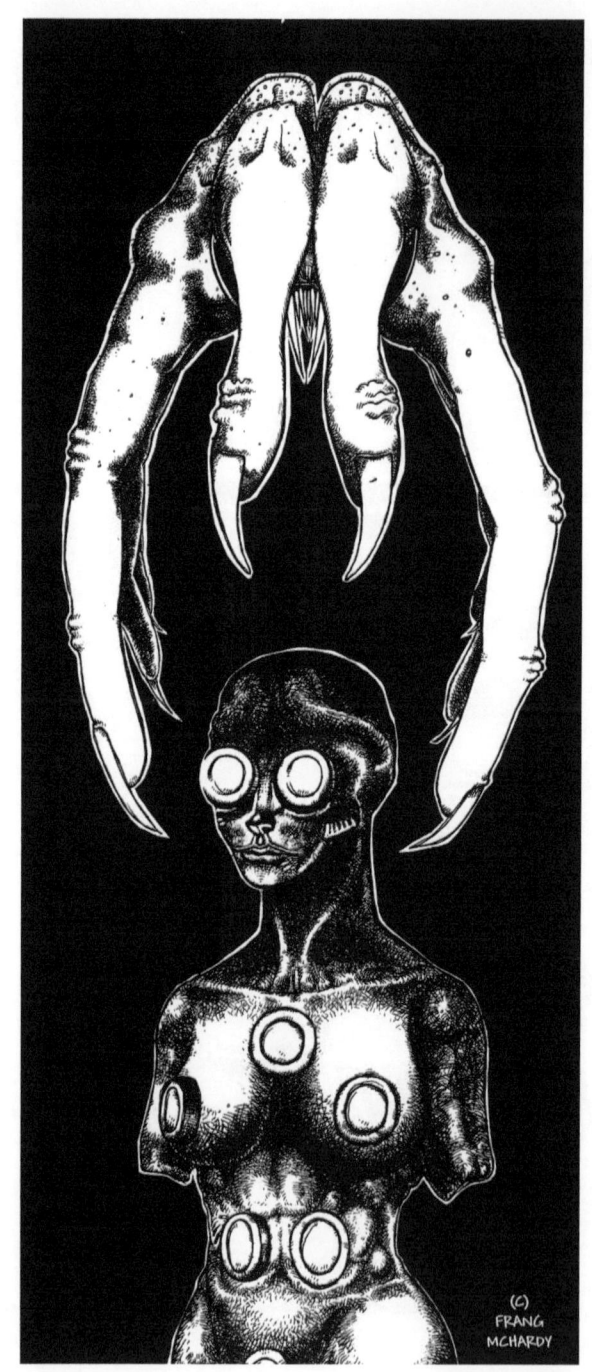

Novice

by

J. I. Stuart

I could sense that there was a bright light shining in my face, and I turned restlessly to avoid it, afraid to open my eyes for fear of what I might see. Memory was hazy, but filled with pain and suffering, and the need to complete a task of the most desperate urgency. I had this awful premonition that the task remained unfulfilled, and I was terrified to face the consequences of having failed a trust. The memory of pain was the most obtrusive - something to do with an ankle? Extreme pain and bright lights added up to hospital. Was I in hospital - if so it was an incredibly silent one. I tentatively tried to check my ankles for pain - I seemed to HAVE no ankles, no legs, no arms.... I could gain no sensations beyond my head! All my former fears vanished as dew in the sun before the much greater terror, and I snapped open my eyes. Or rather I tried to. But the lids were curiously unwilling to obey the relevant commands. Really frightened I opened to mouth to call for help, to shout out my terror and anguish.... Nothing happened! I tried again, and then felt a cool, a cold presence on my forehead, a sweet gentle voice whispered in my ear. It was a calmly reassuring voice that reminded me of a lark on a summer's morning, the sort of voice that one only heard in a dream, and which Callas or Melba would have bartered her soul for.

"Calm down Mark. There's nothing to be frightened of. You're quite safe. In a short time the effects of the.... the medication will start to wear off, and you'll be able to open your eyes, talk, and everything else. Please be patient, just for a little while."

I felt myself relax somewhat, any second expecting to feel a thermometer stuck in between my teeth, but none materialised. I struggled once more to open my eyes, move my lips, but there was still no response, except a recurring panic reaction. What kind of drugs, I asked myself, had I been pumped full of, and why?

It was almost as if the nurse - if nurse she was - had heard my querulous thought.

"It is vital that you remain absolutely still for a few more hours. The operation has been a wonderful success, but to ensure one-hundred percent completion you mustn't move at all. That is why you have been so immobilised - please believe me. Now try and sleep. The time will pass more quickly and easily for you that way."

I tried. But the more I tried, the more my mind spun round in dizzy-making circles, trying to dredge up all the whys and wherefores. I tried to make sense of the events which memory insisted were most recent, running back over them, attempting to impose order on chaos.

Remembered pain, and a task - a machine, a weird machine, an alien machine that had to be.... to be switched off. Terminals that unscrewed the wrong way, racking pains and nausea, crawling, limping, falling.... running and walking.... Why an alien machine? Naked women.... naked alien women in an alien spaceship.... the task. Why the task, where the machine? A spaceship, a big spaceship, an immense spaceship with a personal swimming pool, and no clothes, no shoes - a bed, a vast bed, a comfortable bed. Naked alien women.... a task, a flight, a flying saucer, a meeting.... the meeting and Susie on the common. It clicked into place.

I was Mark John Richards, forty-two, senior systems analyst in the computing department of a large multi-national oil company. I was married with two children and lived in a small village in Yorkshire within reasonable commuting distance of Manchester. I lived in a large rambling Victorian rectory and owned a three year old Sierra which I was thinking of trading in for a new one. I had been taking one of the dogs - Susie, the three year old Labrador bitch - for a walk on the strangely deserted common when it had all started to happen: when I had fallen head first into a fifties science-fiction movie - and a 'B' feature at that.

"Do this small favour for us please?" THEY said.
"Switch off this rogue machine for us," THEY said
"None of us can get near it for the noise," THEY said.
"It'll only take five of your minutes," THEY said.
"I only fell down and broke my bloody ankle of course." So why was I now lying totally immobilised and almost wholly sensory deprived?. It didn't make sense - why a major operation? What harm to be able to talk and open one's eyes? A tantalising memory hovered on the edge - this was not the first time I'd wakened since.... since.... Had the task been completed? Had the machine been switched off? Was I just making everything up - a sort of wish fulfilment dream sequence? Wish fulfilment? Why did I have this feeling that I had actually died, or been dying. There was something there.... something just out of reach.... something that might just explain everything that....

"Come on Mark. Time to wake up. You can open your eyes now if you wish. Soon you'll be able to talk too, and then move - I promise you!"
I had fallen asleep, still reaching for that one memory that persisted in remaining outwith my grasp - the one that would complete the jigsaw. Clearly time had passed. The difference was instantly obvious: I was conscious of lying on a hard surface, my upper half tilted up slightly, head cushioned on some soft resilient surface. An indescribably beautiful voice was speaking to me again. I knew it should be familiar, but no name would sit on it.

I snapped open my eyes, and instantly shut them again. Too, too bright. I re-opened them more cautiously. When I was a schoolboy of sixteen, the school doctor had diagnosed short-sightedness (I'd never wondered why I couldn't see the blackboard that other children had no trouble reading from) and sent me to the optician. After collecting my glasses on the way home from school one day, I had entered an empty house (both parents working, elder sisters left home) and tried the new glasses on in private. I remembered how astonished I'd been to be able to make out every single hair on the coat of my ginger and white cat lying curled up asleep in the arm chair, and being somewhat astonished to realise just how dirty he was - poor little thing. He died on the operating table not very much later on, cancer of the bowel I think the vet meant, though those weren't the words he'd used.

It was like that, opening my eyes - like wearing glasses for they very first time, being able to see properly. I couldn't believe the vibrancy of the colours I was seeing - the multiplicity of the colours, the sharpness of the detail. One hell of an operation! I took a deep breath, and then felt a great wash of fear flood over me - for I hadn't. Hadn't breathed that is! Sounds silly, who (except some invalid with respiration problems, or an athlete at the end of a gruelling competition), is ever really conscious of breathing. I wasn't really, not normally. But I now was very conscious of its absence. That quiet, almost imperceptible flow of air over the palette just was not there any more. I struggled to speak, to say something, but might as well have saved myself the bother. From behind me came that voice again:

"No need to be frightened, it's all perfectly normal."

And strangely enough I was no longer frightened - although the normality of the situation completely escaped me. I concentrated on the voice, but no face would come, so I shifted my attention to the somewhat limited information available to my visual senses. There wasn't very much to see, but what there was, was.... interesting to say the least. Immediately above me was nothing but ceiling - plain, whitish, and so dull as to be absolutely boring, however, further 'down' as it were, towards my feet - assuming that I still possessed such things, was a great sphere hanging suspended in mid air. It glowed and sparkled with an iridescence that made it seem alive - almost like some vast diamond cut into facets so small as to be indistinguishable except to the very rays of light themselves. It seemed to glow and swell, pulsating in and out, until that voice - sharper in tone than hitherto - snapped me out of what could well have become some sort of self-induced hypnoses.

"Think, feel and look - this way Mark." It was a command. I found my eyes automatically swivelling to the right, and a head, a face swam into view - a face that was both beautifully familiar, yet unknown. A name surfaced, then two, and a third: Denella, Jastie, Jeftie.... None seemed to fit, or even be quite right in themselves somehow. The voice, now firmly attached to the face - both smiling, continued:

"No, we haven't met before. I am J'sati. Strictly it should have been D'nelaa who would have been here when you woke, but some kind of crisis blew up - and I was deputised to welcome you back."

I briefly tried to say something simple - 'Hello' or whatever, but there was no noticeable response from my lips, throat and whatever, so instead I repeated the name over to myself: 'Jusaty....' and compared it with the three syllables I'd heard. Not quite right. 'Jesartie....' No, that was worse. 'Jay-sa-tie?'

"It's J'sati." The vision interrupted my musings, with a trilling of amusement only just evident in the liquid tones, "Jay dash, or maybe an apostrophe would be more appropriate, then Ess, Ay, Tee, Eye."

I had tried it out for size and approved the amendment when the sense of her words struck home. Coincidence? I sighed internally, what would I not give for a little more information on where I was - the power to ask questions, to know what was happening, had happened, who was what, where why when, and.... and...."

"That's quite a lot of questions. Any specific order?"

I could feel my mind start to explode as the chilling significance of her words struck home - there could be no doubt whatsoever: she knew precisely what I was thinking, every thought that passed through my brain was hers to play with and....

Then it was as if a bucket of water had quenched the explosion - stillborn. Another concept struggled to emerge from the backwaters of my head, but it too was snuffed out before I could grasp hold of it.

"A lot to take in, I know," she continued smoothly, "But If it's any consolation, I should perhaps say that it's only your very surface thoughts that are available for inspection. A little practice and control and anything you want really concealed will be truly hidden." Her tone implied that a truly integrated and honest personality would have little to so hide away.

'I believe you,' I thought back at her, wondering if irony was detectable as a surface concept, *'Forgive me if I take a little time to get used to the idea.'*

"Oh that's quite all right. We've plenty of time. And irony IS detectable, by the way." Manfully I tried to force the inevitable cheap retort into a 'lower' level of consciousness, and apparently nearly succeeded: "Oh that was good - you're learning very quickly indeed. I had to probe quite deep in order to catch that one. Excellent. It took me very much longer than that to get even half as far."

That was a bit of a puzzler. I formulated my next thought rather carefully: *'Are you trying to tell me that this.... this mind reading business is a new thing for you too?'*

"Well no and yes. No, it's been the standard method of communication amongst us Klylii for as long as we can remember - several thousand million years anyway - but as regards me personally, yes: I mean, I'm only a child after all."

'Only a child!' How to deflate an ego in one short sentence. *'I see. All the adults are otherwise engaged eh?'*

"Yes, that's right. As I mentioned earlier, some crisis blew up, and as the eldest, I was deputised to oversee your.... awakening."

'Well, that's something I suppose. How old are you? Or is that an impolite question.'

"Oh no. I'm.... twenty-seven."

Twenty Seven? I pondered briefly. Must be some odd unit of time peculiar to the Klylii themselves. *'Twenty-seven whats?'*

"Why years - Earth years of course."

'You're twenty-seven - a child! When do you grow up, for goodness sake?'

"Oh not long now. Another three, four, maybe five years. It depends on progress.... and various other factors." She must have been sitting down, for suddenly her head rose some two feet vertically upwards, and I was granted a view of her upper body, almost down to the waist - it didn't look very immature. She clearly caught my involuntary reaction.

"Oh I'm fully mature physically - have been for oh, ten, fifteen years now. It's the mind that takes the time to grow up properly."

'Ah. Of course. All this thought transference business. Silly of me.'

"That's right. And it's not silly at all. How could you possibly know without being told."

'I see. So it takes you fifteen years or so to learn how to read thoughts out of the surface of a mind. Must be a very difficult process.'

"Well - there's more to it than just that of course."

'More to what - reading minds?'

"No. More to growing up, mentally. Young Klylii have all sorts of things to learn, many skills to develop and practice." She didn't expand on that bald statement, though she must have known I was expecting her to. Instead she sat herself down again, but must have moved her seat somewhat nearer for she ended up much closer to me than before. A whole list of questions suddenly re-surfaced out of the depths of my mind, making me almost forget my curiosity

'I understand I've been through a major operation. Why? And why aren't I apparently breathing. Why am I not just immobilised, but unable to feel anything below the neck? Why?'

J'sati's eyes momentarily seemed to lose focus - I would probably have missed it but for the fact that there was nothing else to look at, and it was a very look-at-able face indeed. It lasted a second, no more, the animation returning almost instantly,

"Tell me...." She shifted herself even closer, "Does the idea of death frighten you?"

'Death!' I went through the mental process which would normally have resulted in a gulp. 'I can't say it frightens me any more than any other unknown. I think it's probably just the idea of knowing in advance, of wondering if there will be great personal pain attached, and what the effect will be on one's loved ones left behind. And maybe also the fact that it's so final. Most other things are more or less reversible, if the will exists.'

"I see. And do you hold any particular views about a 'Life after Death'? I understand that a very large number of.... of humans hold religious beliefs which include 'Heavens', 'Hells', reincarnation, and various other concepts."

'Not overtly so - I think. I'm sure that everyone of us, at some time or another, has secretly hoped that perhaps the end may just be a beginning, but I can't say that there appears to have been any really supporting evidence to suggest that death is anything other than dissolution. Seems a waste that a complex intelligence with a lifetime of experience and memories should just fade away, like the RAM of a computer when it's powered down, but I suppose the idea is that one teaches one's children to learn by your mistakes - except that they never seem to.' A sudden memory flashed into being, 'You, or someone else asked me something like that before.' A whole section of recollections suddenly lay exposed and vulnerable. I picked through them swiftly. Pain, suffering, agonies of mind and body from which death would have been blessed relief - and a question of reincarnation.

"Yes. That was D'nelaa."

'Denella?' I was momentarily diverted.

"D'nelaa: Dee, apostrophe, Enn, Ee, Ell, Ay, Ay."

'D'nelaa. Quite so. Why?'

She made no pretence to have misunderstood me, but for the first time turned her head away from me, and I was granted an enchanting profile. "It was basically a matter of ethics," She said, her beautiful voice very slightly muffled. "You were dying. We needed to obtain your conscious permission to.... to carry out the.... the operation. Not one with a very high degree of success attached to it I might add."

'You mean there was a high risk of death attached to the operation?'
"No. I said you were dying. You did. You died - absolutely, just like your IBM PC does when you pull the plug out of the wall. What we needed, was your permission to.... to dump the memory on to.... on to a.... another machine, as it were."

I think I must have nearly blacked out. My mind went into a sort of high speed spin, a wild oscillation: *'Untrue, impossible - I'm me, Mark Richards, always have been, you can't move personalities about like a bunch of chessmen....'*

I surfaced to find J'sati leaning closely over me, what had to be a concerned expression in those great glowing amber eyes. As I opened my eyes to stare up at her, her expression lightened somewhat and she drew back fractionally.

"Quite true," She said calmly, "What sort of a creature do you think I would be to tell lies, make jokes about something so fundamental as that."

I made to swallow, to draw a deep breath, and noted that there seemed slight responsive muscular movements. I put the fact temporarily aside and concentrated on J'sati's words:

'So....' The question had to be asked. Might as get it over. I continued her own analogy. *'.... what kind of machine did I get?'*

"Oh.... well I think it's a pretty good model by and large. Only one careful owner, you might say. A fairly versatile piece of equipment." She stood up. "Very similar to this one that you're looking at right now!"

I did lose consciousness at that point. Whether I fainted, or was anaesthetised by some kindly agency, I never asked. And J'asti didn't volunteer the information. I understand I was out for about six hours, and when I awoke found that all the feelings I was used to, and which had temporarily been denied me, had returned - albeit with a sort of subtle difference.

I opened my eyes. I was lying flat on my back, and found I was staring up at a domed ceiling, tastefully decorated in a pastel blue shade which met at an elaborate cornice, a continuous elliptical wall - decorated in a slightly darker shade of blue - which was broken by two graceful archways.... The strange glittering globe had gone. I was back in the place (room was too mundane a word) where I had spent my first night off my home planet.

The disposition of the contents of the bed-chamber were as I remembered them. I was much more interested in the equipment nearer at hand. I held 'my' hands up in front of my face, examined the palms and backs. So smooth: no sign of any pores; no wrinkles; the very, very faintest of fine, fine down could just be seen when viewed at certain angles that lent a delicately whitish tinge to the pale green. There was no trace of underlying veins to be seen. I gently flexed the long slender fingers, noting how the skin seemed to stretch to accommodate the movements, rather than un-wrinkling. The finger nails were very narrow and ridged, almost but not quite claws, a dark orange in colour and hooked over slightly into blunt points. The fingers seemed to move much more easily than human digits, and I found I could, with ridiculous ease, tap out six different beats simultaneously on the fingers of one hand.

My eyes travelled up my arm and flitted across to rest on my chest. A fine pair - E cup at least, but firmer, rounder than would be found on a normal human woman of such dimensions. I tentatively cupped one in my hand and confirmed the diagnosis. A close look at the nipple suggested that they could well have been designed to perform the same function as their human equivalents. Almost frightened by the implications, I moved on, bending forward to examine somewhat further afield, and discovered that the torso was remarkably flexible, my examination being temporarily diverted by a great mass of orange hair falling forward over my face, virtually obscuring everything. I swept it back out of the way holding most of it in place with one hand, noting almost absently how fine and silky it felt, and explored another region of dense orange hair, that which engirdled my hips, like a short built-in grass skirt. Noting in passing that I had nothing that even remotely resembled a navel, I tentatively investigated that area so neatly covered by its silky fringe, wondering, almost guiltily what secrets it might conceal, and feeling strangely relieved but also puzzled to discover - nothing. Nothing at all. I slid off the bed and had approached the mirror before I was fully aware of having performed the act. There was a sort of superb automatic overall co-ordination of effort, of cause and effect, that made one almost unaware of even possessing a body to move around. In an erect position, legs slightly splayed, I surveyed and prodded more thoroughly. It was quite true. The fringe merely concealed a very short length of thigh and a bit of the lower torso. Between the thighs there was smooth seamless skin - no bodily orifices of any kind that I could discover.

I sat back on the bed, and absently contemplated a pair of long slender legs which (apart from the colour) any stripper would have given her eye-teeth to own. Clearly the close outward resemblance between Humanity and The Klylii was little more than that - a close outward resemblance. I stood up again and examined the hauntingly beautiful face which topped the body now inhabited by my ego. The eyes, lips, mouth interior of tongue and teeth etcetera, the nose, ears and everything, all appeared reasonably normal, but than what was normal to a systems analyst could well send a doctor or biologist into wild frenzies of delight. I just did not know enough to be able to comment sensibly one way or another, human specialisation having reached such a pitch of stupidity....

I sat down again, absently pushing the shoulder length hair back out of the way again and bent forward to examine my hips area once more, especially the way the engirdling fringe seemed to grow out.... I carefully ran a finger tip along the edge of the hairline and discovered a skin flap stretching from hip to hip forming what could only be a pouch, like that on a kangaroo, or wallaby.

I stood up again, and walked backwards and forwards across the breath of the room trying to detect.... what? A strangeness? An alien-ness? There was a difference

- no way could I claim otherwise - but it was a sort of familiar difference, and I stopped my pacing to stand still once more, facing the mirror. I pushed my hair back off my face with both hands and stood there, hands just touching each other round the back of my neck, and stared long and hard at the reflected image, willing it to sink in, to become reality and second nature.

Later - much later - I was given detailed technical description of the process that had been used to transfer my consciousness from one body to another - from the near corpse of a human male to that of the mindless relic of a tragic accident. I can't say I really understood it at the time. That kind of biological detail just wasn't my forte. H'dasa herself had owned to being bafflingly amazed at the effectiveness of a series of procedures that, especially towards the end, had been little more than a string of more or less desperate measures introduced largely by guess and a gut instinctive feel as the race against total dissolution grew ever more fraught. She'd confided that after the incredibly haphazard and drawn out procedure had finally guttered to its inevitable end with, She had been convinced at the time, a shortfall of some fifteen percent, She had disconsolately left the area convinced that it had been a total failure, very little consoled by the realities of the situation and the assurances of everyone that the donor had just been too far gone *'I should have done more basic research lamast since.'* She'd castigated, as J'sfti tried to console her. *'Been more ready for such an occurrence. Why else did we bother to preserve H'orlaa's body?'*

'One can only do one's best - and no one could have done more than you H'dasa'

'That's what I try to tell myself, but I can't help wondering if perhaps....'

It was at about that point that D'nella had excitedly announced that there were sign of a stabilising acceptance, and despite every early indication to the contrary, the translated consciousness began to establish itself ever more firmly.

'It was quite incredible' H'dasa had confided. *'After we knew that it had worked, after J'sati had reported just how well you were doing, I went away and did all the theory that I would have loved to have done before the "operation". And do you know what the odds were? There weren't any not really. I'd been right after all. According to the theory it shouldn't have worked: the transfer should by rights have failed.'*

'Very heartening,' had been my comment

'Oh don't be depressed.' H'dasa had hastened to reassure me, *'I think it was just one of those situations were there was an overwhelming will to succeed - on everyone's part that just over-rode all technical considerations.'*

'I see. Still, I suppose the experience was worth it. You'll know now what not to do if anything similar ever crops up in the future.'

'Unfortunately not. The one thing I learnt - despite its overwhelming success in your case - is that successful personality transfer is not done the way I thought it should. It's back to the beginning again, and I have to confess that I don't really know which way to go.'

I'd never been a particularly lucky person, never winning a raffle in my life, despite all the tickets I'd bought over the years, and regularly losing at cards. But I suppose one had to get a break sooner or later and one big slice of luck could make up for it all. It looked like, when it mattered, the dice had finally fallen my way at last.

I was still there, in front of the mirror, as if frozen in position an unknown quantity of time later, when J'sati arrived. Perhaps she could detect what I was doing and had become concerned over the inordinate length of time I was spending motionless, and perhaps she had merely left me alone for some pre-determined period of time. Movement in the mirror alerted me to her presence behind me, and I swung round. I opened my mouth to say something, anything, but she held up a finger and I sensed a sort of feeling of negation emanating from her. There was a curious sensation within my head, like a sort of soundless, visionless crackling and flashing of bright lights. It was almost as if I were thinking the thoughts myself, but knew I wasn't:

'No audible speech please. Let us start as we must continue. Communication via direct thought transference is a very simple process, with amazingly complex variations. The sooner the basic principles are FULLY mastered, the swifter everything else will fall into place.'

'I don't really think....'

'No. Or rather yes. That's precisely what you're doing: thinking, only thinking. You must PROJECT the concepts outwards, towards me.'

'How? Like this?'

'Better. Push harder. Concentrate more.... Narrow it down, finer.... That's better. And as you see, we can both "talk" at the same time. Duplex transmission. But you're doing the equivalent of shouting at the top of your voice - half the ship would be cowering at the blast if they weren't politely ignoring it. Try toning it down somewhat - a sort of whispering.... Much improved.... a little more.... Good, very good.'

The lesson lasted a full two hours. Then there came the lecture.

'Direct interchange of information, mind to mind is, as I implied much earlier, a simple business with complex variations - VERY complex variations. There are many different levels, or intensities of linking, each deeper level granting access to more profound areas of the mind. Such joining together of one mind to another is called Communion. It's a temporary merging of identities and can be almost as profound and meaningful as the protagonists desire. The ultimate form is a complete and total fusion of personalities, known as Conjunction - wholly irreversible, of course.'

'Irreversible? Total fusion of personalities? I'm not sure I fully understand.'

'One mind inhabiting two bodies.'

'One mind inhabiting.... I think we'll come back to that one later.'

'Good idea. Even living with one - My Parent, parents, doesn't make Her, them, any easier to understand. That only comes with time and experience of which I have little, and you none.'

'True, although I must admit I'm amazed at how calmly I seem to be taking all this. If asked previously, I would have imagined it to be an infinitely more traumatic experience than would appear to have actually been the case.'

J'sati looked down at her feet, avoiding my glance. *'It's not actually.'*

'Not what?'

'Been quite as calm and unconcerned as you imagine.'

'I don't quite follow you.'

There was an imperceptible pause - a sort of break in transmission - before she continued. *'The brain of a Klylii is a complicated structure, slightly larger than its human equivalent - and a good bit more massive. The cell structure is finer being some three times smaller than a human brain and is also more efficient in operation and with the neurons being closer together can form much more complex links. The end result gives the Klylii access to many thousands of times more 'brain' than even the smartest Earthman that ever lived. Much of that extra capacity is used up controlling the higher level functions, and a good bit is also tied up in the Racial Memory.'* I was flabbergasted. Too amazed to even think of making any kind of return. She went on. *'All those areas have, in you, been temporarily blanked off - for obvious reasons. You would go swiftly insane trying to make sense of just a tiny portion of the available information - at the present. What you are using now is a very small fraction of brain that roughly corresponds to what was available to you in your old body, with a little bit extra, otherwise, of course, you would be wholly unaware of what I was telling you.'*

She turned around to look directly at me. *'And I must also confess that even that is not wholly accurate. There are certain small parts of your mind, parts of the residual human section, to which access is also barred - I am barring your access. Were I not, you would be nothing like so calm as you are: indeed the word hysterical would be something of a euphemism. In time of course, that control will be relaxed and finally withdrawn as your mind gradually becomes more accustomed to its new surroundings - probably about a week should be enough.'*

I tried to be furious with her for mucking around with my natural thought processes and emotions - surely I had a right to go stark staring bonkers if I wished - but found I couldn't: doubtless one of the fenced off areas. And on mature reflection decided that perhaps it was only fair that things be given a reasonable chance to settle in. I remembered all the stratagems we'd been to forced to adopt a year or so ago in order to prevent Susie from licking open the stitches left after her operation, and all for the beast's own good. I considered the implications of what I'd just learnt. Racial Memory? I ducked that one for the time.

'Higher level functions? Plural? Is there some significance there?'

'Yes.' She didn't elaborate.

'Well! Don't I get to know? Is that something for later?'

'No. Oh no. I was just trying to work out the best way of putting things.' There was a hiatus then, *'Over there - on the table beneath the mirror.'* I looked in the indicated place and saw that a perfectly normal looking hairbrush was floating in mid air about a foot above the dressing table top. As I watched, eyes bulging (in thought, if not in fact) it turned and sailed placidly over towards us, straight onto J'asti's outstretched palm. Her fingers closed around the handle and she waved it gently to and fro before tossing it lightly (through a perfectly normal parabola) on to the bed. *'That's one higher level function.'* The figure seated on the bed beside me abruptly vanished,

to instantly re-appear standing beside the dressing table. *'And this is another.'* Suddenly she was back on the bed again, on my LEFT hand side though, rather than on my right where she'd been a second before. Had I been in the business of breathing I daresay several deep breaths would have resulted.

'I.... I see.' I replied what must have been somewhat shakily. *'Very handy on a ship the size of this one I should imagine - or are there limitations?'*

'Yes.' She had shifted herself back to her original position on my right. I suppose one could get used to anything. *'But they're not intrinsic. The limits vary according to the health, experience and development progress of the individual, the available energy sources, and several other factors. And again one has to be practical, because the transfer involves a fair degree of effort, especially if one is raising oneself any appreciable distance in a gravity field. Although the actual transfer takes no time at all, one has to be absolutely precise over one's starting and finishing points. That involves a skill we call "Assessment" and does takes time. Under normal circumstances, any distances under about fifty yards one would generally walk unless there was some real urgency. In the same way that you would never have dreamed of getting out the car in order to post a letter.'*

'Ah.... Quite so. This "assessment" I presume is another Higher Level Function.'

'Yes. It basically is a means of directly perceiving the physical world, and is, as you probably guessed, also needed to fetch hairbrushes off tables without getting out of bed. It also allows one to examine any object thoroughly in as much detail as is necessary, down to sub-atomic levels if required.'

'Fascinating. Any other surprises to spring?'

'That's about it. Though there's a sort of survival factor that operates between siblings and is wholly independent of distance or anything else that warns if the other is in extreme danger.'

'I hardly think that's likely to be of much interest to me.'

'Would you be surprised to learn that you have three.... sisters?'

'I suppose I should, but as all my emotions are under your firm grip, you must know the answer to that one. Anyway, is it proper to refer to them as such?'

'Oh yes. Perfectly right and proper. And that brings up another question: Your name.'

'My name? What about my name?

'Well however suitable a handle like "Mark John Richards" may be in the wilds of West Yorkshire, it doesn't really go here. We're going to have to come up with something a bit more succinct, something with rather more meaning.'

I think it was that; J'sati's matter of fact mention of names and the need to change it, that really brought it all home to me in a way that even standing in front of the mirror hadn't. IT HAD ACTUALLY HAPPENED! It was all real.... real.... REAL! I was no longer me, but something so totally different that I couldn't even be allowed to know just big that difference was! For a short time the room and everything in it faded from consciousness as I grappled with the implications. I was no longer Mark Richards, no longer a man, no longer even human. It was authentic - and permanent!

'Feeling a trifle better?'

I managed to pull myself together. *'Yes. Yes, I'm fine thanks. Sorry about that. Delayed reaction or something I should imagine.'*

'Or something. I just released one of the blocks. You came through it very well. Better than I'd expected.

'Ah. I suppose I'd better expect similar occurrences for quite a while.'

'Sort of. Best without warning though - believe me. Anyway, names!'

'Names it is. Do I get a choice or anything. Do Klylii names have any meaning attached?'

'Of course. Don't human ones?'

'They did originally. The forenames meant abstract things like Strength, and Justice, Beauty or Loyalty, and so forth. The surnames generally related to occupations or where one lived, or who one's father had been or something. But it's all pretty academic these days: a number would do just as well; and to most organisations, one IS a number. And they're all different. Most confusing.'

'So it would appear.' There was a brief pause, then she continued, *'The name of the personality who's body you now inhabit used to be H'orlaa. And I must say that she was half of a Pair called H'uolaa. The other physical half, H'ures, was sadly blown to atoms in an unfortunate accident, and as you can imagine the shock of suddenly loosing half her mind, was instantly fatal to the remainder of the personality. The empty shell has been carefully preserved ever since against just such an eventuality as has now occurred. As regards the significance of names - there's not much point in going particularly deeply into all that yet, suffice it to say that each name consists of three parts. The first section, the initial "letter" if you like, the bit preceded by the apostrophe is a sign of.... rank I suppose is the best way to describe it. The highest ranking possible is "K" - reserved for our Kaelyj Herself - Emperor or Empress is probably the closest analogy - followed by "J", lines up with King or Queen I suppose, then "H", "G", "F", "D" and "C" in descending order. The next one, two or three "'letters" make up the personal name, and the last two or three constitute the family name. Thus my name, J'sati splits into "Sa" personal name, and "Ti" family name which, naturally, comes from my Parent, J'sfti. The J' part of my name is merely a courtesy until I'm fully mature, borrowed from my Parent. Once I've been Called, and Assigned, I shall be Graded as appropriate. And will probably be lucky to make an F' ranking.'*

'It sounds fairly straightforward as far as it goes, but what do "Called", "Assigned" and "Graded" mean?'

'Every ten years or so - sometimes more often, sometimes less frequently depending on circumstances, Consensus is held; an occasion where everyone gets together and the business of the Race is carried out. It's a fully integrated third level mass Communion - where everything is revealed. It's impossible to conceal any infractions of the code - even assuming one wished to try. Everything of importance or interest that's occurred since the last Consensus is freely commented on, weighted,

evaluated and general consensus arrived at. Individuals who have performed well are publicly praised by their seniors and subordinates - perhaps promoted in rank - that is, be Re-Graded. The reverse can also happen, but not very often. Sometimes there may have been someone who has transgressed the Code - possibly with very good reason - but the Code is the Code, and standards must be maintained, and discipline may be needed. Also, as circumstances alter, and people develop and change, some may be recommended for or seek a different class of speciality or official occupation - known as a Re-Assignment.'

My head was spinning, grappling with the concept of an entire race in continuous overall mental communication. She continued:

'After all the serious business is over, then any juveniles who have "Come-of-Age" since last Consensus are then "Called Into Consensus". That is, officially brought into full adult race membership, and are "Assigned" an occupation - profession or job if you like - and "Graded" according to ability as determined from one's Parent, teachers and so on. After that the Racial Memory is updated and then the whole thing turns into a party - Klylii style. It probably wouldn't look much to an outsider.'

My mind was a jumble of confused emotions and concepts that required careful sorting and appraisal, but she rushed on.

'However, we're straying from the point. That of a selecting a name for you. You should retain the original family name - unless there's a very strong objection - and the base rank until called. So it's just a matter of choosing a familiar or personal name. Obviously you can't use one already belonging to someone else, and without access to the Racial Memory you can't know what's available, or their meanings.'

'I see.' At least I thought I did. *'This body. You say the original personality went by the name of H'orlaa. How much of the "Orlaa" was family, and how much personal?'*

'She was a member of the important "Laa" family - more Kaelyjs have come from it than any other three families taken together. And some families have quite a tradition of leadership, my own "Ti" family included.'

'So her familiar name was "Or". What did it mean?'

J'sati's eyes glazed over slightly, and she froze momentarily, as had happened several times before. I wondered if perhaps she were consulting someone else - questioning her "Parent" or other senior. It lasted, as ever, barely a second or so before she gave me the answer:

'It's something on the lines of a term of endearment meaning: "Latest and dearly loved addition." H'orlaa was the youngest of four - a large close family: two is normally as many as most Pairs ever produce - one is probably even more common. You understand that we have to be careful over our breeding patterns so as not to overpopulate our world.'

'Very sensible - would other races acted as responsibly. What's the average Klylii life span?' I asked, and as a natural, corollary, *'How old was.... H'orlaa when.... it.... happened.'*

'She was about forty....'

Forty. That was fair and reasonable, I supposed. If one only became fully mature at about thirty, then on a reasonable analogy I could expect about.... J'sati interrupted my mathematical perambulations:

'.... lamasts. That's roughly thirteen hundred Earth years. No age at all really, though She was one of the oldest aboard ship - a full Counsellor of course. Why K'laa, our Kaelyj is.... twenty-eight thousand years old, and there are many others a good bit older than that. It's not something that holds all that much importance.'

'Twenty-eight thousand years old!' My mind was in a flat spin, *'And you say there are others older?*

'Oh yes. Four, five, maybe ten times. Difficult to say really.'

I gulped. Or tried to. I think I managed the mental equivalent, struggling to get a grip on a spiralling imagination that appeared to be wholly dwarfed by reality. *'So what's the theoretical life span then,'* I asked again, surely very faintly indeed.

Something akin to a shrug came across - the first real clue I'd received that thought transference could be any more than the simple verbalising of concepts between participants, and suddenly it was as if I could see past the edge of a door - open a bare crack - to glimpse the wonders in a summer garden outside. Frustrating, to say the least. Maybe J'sati had removed another little block.

'Nobody knows. I can't say for sure of course lacking access to the Racial Memory, but I don't think a death from old age has ever been recorded. We all tend to die in accidents and so forth, as happened to the original H'orlaa's conjugate half, H'ures.'

'Ah yes. Poor H'orlaa.' My mind was settling down somewhat. Perhaps possession of all these super senses wasn't quite such a great deal after all. Maybe it was possible to be so busy lining oneself up to teleport across town that one neglected to watch out for the bus coming up behind you - metaphorically speaking. I wondered what kind of tragic accident had snuffed out H'ures. What had J'sati said earlier? Blown apart? Not something on which one really wished to dwell for too long. It would have been quick though. Have to quick of course. No other way possible when one came to consider it. H'orlaa: Latest and dearly loved addition. I wondered how she would have felt to know that one time.... *'Presumably I wouldn't be allowed to use the same name would I?'* I asked somewhat diffidently. *'I suppose that would be resented by her family, and create all sorts of confusion in the records department.'*

'You would like to use the same name? H'orlaa?

'Is it possible?'

'Of course.'

'It wouldn't cause problems? Her family wouldn't mind?'

'They will be touched and gratified. After all, consider the realities of the case: they are YOUR family now.... H'orlaa.'

It was as simple as that. And it was that simple thing, that made the reality of what had happened to me FULLY come home. I stood up as if in a trance and walked across to the mirror again: H'orlaa. I had somehow become a member of a race of immortal super beings, and my name was H'orlaa. A minute, an hour, a day later -

who was counting - I surfaced to find J'sati gone. She had slipped away, quietly, unnoticed to leave me alone with my feelings.

She returned not very long afterwards, just when I had managed to make some kind of sense out of and do some sifting and sorting of the incredible information she'd carelessly thrown my way earlier. I had a sort of premonition of her coming, and was waiting, watchfully alert, as she abruptly appeared at my side.

'Greetings J'sati.' The welcome seemed to spring unbidden to the forefront of my mind.

'And best greetings to you H'orlaa,' was the response. I felt a strange but not unpleasant shiver run through me. She continued, *'It would appear that you have used the past few asts to good purpose. Excellent. Your progress is well ahead of that expected.'*

'It is? I briefly considered what I'd been told and balanced the infinitesimal portion I'd advanced against what must lie ahead - even forgetting the empty gaps yet to be filled in, and despaired somewhat. *'How long do you expect it to take before.... I'm even half competent. And what is an 'Ast'?'*

'Probably at least ten amasts. And an ast is a unit of time. I'll give you a conversion table if you wish. Though it's not the best way to think of such things in the long term, I suppose it can do little harm at this stage. Soon though you must start to reason from basic elementals.'

The conversion table she gave me looked something like:

1	Sun	6 nanoseconds
1	Time Unit (Un)	0.8 microseconds
1	Mun	115 microseconds
1	Amun	17 milliseconds
1	Lamun	2.4 seconds
1	Ast	6 minutes
1	Mast	14 hours
1	Amast	83 days (3 months)
1	Lamast	33 years
1	Eun	5000 years

and I studied it briefly. Ten amasts equated to some two and a half years. It was a not unreasonable time when one considered just how much would have to be learned. I tried to imagine some alien creature suddenly arriving in the middle of late twentieth century Britain and having to learn the entire culture. I tried to imagine a stone-age man, a Tudor man, even a Victorian man being bounced forward in time - awakening from stasis - and trying to adapt to the Nineteen-nineties. I recalled the tales that Mark Richard's wife Janet had told him about the old residents in the nursing home where she worked - even they, who had grown up in the society had largely lost touch with it: I remembered being confused by current slang used by teenagers, on television.

A society is a dynamic organisation. Even moving from one section of planet Earth to another was a traumatic experience from which some never recovered, even without something as simple as a language difference to overcome - witness the high proportion of British emigrants who returned to the UK from Australia, Canada, America, even after years of living in that country, never having really felt at home, having completely fitted in. Both Mark and Janet had examples of that very thing in their families - a sister and an aunt who had finally given up the unequal struggle.

But for me - H'orlaa - there could be no going back. It was integrate or die, for there could be no middle road. Two and a.... I caught myself up and laid the sheet of white card face down on the bed. Ten amasts was not a very long time. In fact it was an incredibly brief period. Still, I DID have all the necessary equipment. I briefly touched my hair, then smoothed my hands down over my breasts, hips, thighs, and carefully seated myself. *'Induction lesson part two I presume?'*

She joined me. *'Something like that. Questions? You must have some, or would you rather I gave you a brief history lesson, a sort of skeletal outline into which everything can later be fitted?'*

'History lesson please.'

'Good.' There was the briefest of pauses. *'The Klylii don't go in much for written records - everything of importance is all there in the Racial Memory - instantly accessible to any and every adult. It is, I believe - for of course I myself have as yet no first hand experience of it - somewhat vague over exact time-scales. A fault from which written records also suffer without an absolute reference system of course. I emphasise this so you'll realise that the periods I mention are approximate only.'*

'Ah yes. Give or take a few hundred euns eh?'

'That's right.' My attempt at humour badly misfired, *'Or a few thousand. Anyway,'* she continued, *'The Race which calls itself The Klylii, originated, or so it is believed, on the planet Klyl, a good while ago - we've certainly lived there for a long time - some scholars estimate it to be in excess of a million euns. I am not competent to judge. Certainly we are an extremely old race - one that of necessity breeds very slowly due to the long individual lifespans of its members. Those you meet aboard this ship are not typical: they are the restless young ones, the inquisitive young ones, the reckless young ones, the clever young ones. That is why out of a crew of around a hundred there are no less than TWELVE children. I know, in human terms that spells extinction, but on Klyl such a ratio is unknown, totally unthinkable for there, the average community of ten thousand - assuming such a term could be properly be used to describe how we live on our home world - would be more likely NOT to include a child than otherwise.'*

She gave me a few moments for that to sink in before continuing

'We haven't had space travel for very long - less than three euns - and there were many who opposed the whole idea right from the start - more so after the first ship crashed on its fourth landfall killing most of the crew. It took nearly twenty lamasts for the survivors to build a new ship to take them back home. Most of them are still there. But the younger ones, those born in space or on that ill-fated planet, where

so much was lost and so much achieved, against all advice built a third ship incorporating all their hard won expertise, this one, and again ventured forth to explore the wider Universe. It's been voyaging ever since.'

A voyage: one crew, one ship - already twelve thousand years old. And no suspended animation in sight. A crew which confidently expected once more to walk on their Race's home world. Just how long would the trip last - twenty millennium, thirty? The name of the game seemed to be adjustment: wider still and wider, let nothing hold back the imagination, for there are no bounds.

'Are you..... Are we voyaging with any purpose?' I eventually queried.

'Perhaps. If my Parent has such at heart She has yet to inform me, Her youngest of such a plan. I suspect that most, if not all of our shipmates simply like wandering around the Galaxy looking at what other races get up to.'

'Are there many other such Civilisations about?'

'Enough to make it interesting. We try and keep notes on the various planets visited in order to see just how well (or otherwise) the inhabitants are progressing. We visited Earth way back in the beginning. In fact.... it was actually Earth on which the original ship crashed about two and a half euns - twelve thousand human years ago. We tried to be as inconspicuous as possible, impinge upon the primitive inhabitants minimally, but let's face it, its very hard to build a kilometre high spaceship in secret. Of course the whole planet was very sparsely populated. I don't suppose more than a handful of tribes ever noticed our presence - and they were probably much too busy surviving to bother about us. It was quite a hectic period I understand. Earth was just emerging from an ice-age'

I briefly considered the surprising information given me as an aside almost. Ten thousand BC. Definitely Stone Age stuff. She was probably right about the almost total lack of impact. Oh, various authors had postulated that the pyramids of Egypt and Central America had been inspired by alien spaceships, but they talked so much utter rubbish generally..... J'sati continued, cutting across my deliberations

There are surprisingly enough, very few races with space-flight, even up to the rudimentary standards currently achieved by the Human Race. Some of our keenest researchers are of the opinion that space-flight, nuclear energy, and social disruption tend to arrive virtually simultaneously, and that it takes exceptional skills to progress past that point without either moral or physical disintegration - the one in all likelihood triggering off the other... '

I had to agree with her. Much as it saddened me to admit it, there was no doubt that Earth was approaching both flat out. J'sati consoled me. *'Don't feel too badly over your.... former people, H'orlaa. There are reasons to believe that they may well actually have passed the point of maximum danger. That is not to say that dissolution is impossible - far from it - but the worst period was probably the nineteen seventies. Of course most of their trouble stems from the ridiculous form of government employed by the better half of the planet. Not that there is anything intrinsically WRONG with a democracy, so long as one has the sense to elect a leader strong enough to convince the people that what it.... he or she can do for the people is* what the people most need and want. The other trick is to prevent that leader from getting delusions of grandeur. I remember my Parent telling me that they - before they Paired - once went on a landing expedition to a particular planet - I forget the name, if we ever discovered what it was. Poor J'asti was shot at, denounced as a witch, and finally exorcised - fortunately in her absence, and I don't know what. It was very lucky for her that J'efti was actually some distance away at the time of the attack, but close enough to be able to create a diversion long enough to bring the lander in for a rescue.'

J'sati had actually gone on to give a greater explanation as to just why J'asti couldn't simply teleport herself out of the problem, or put the warring natives all to sleep, but it passed me by. I had seized on a particularly significant item of information, that was causing my sorely tried thinking apparatus to make yet more adjustments. *'Your parents are J'efti and J'asti?'* I queried at length. She halted in full flow.

'J'sfti? Yes. That's right. Surely I explained that way back, not long after you first woke

'Yes. But not that J'sfti was the same Person as J'efti and J'asti.'

'Oh. Yes well. But even on Earth..... . I explained about names, remember? The 'J' prefi:. Surely you must have realised that there can only ever be the one "Queen" in the Ship at any one time?'

'I... um... I suppose I Simply failed to associate the names with...' I was giving only a fraction of my mind to what I was saying. Something much more important was crowding its way into the forefront of my thinking apparatus.

'You mean,' I could barely formulate the concepts, so alien was it to my whole life's experience. *'That ALL Klylii look like this?'* I indicated myself, paying particular attention to the chest area. *'Both sexes look the same - identical?'*

'Not just look.'

'You mean... ARE the same!?'

'But of course. Even on Earth there are a sufficient variety of species to indicate that bi-sexuality is hardly the be-all and end-all of existence. The Universe abounds with almost as many different methods of reproduction as there are different races.'

'You could be right. Unfortunately I took chemistry and physics at school - I don't think it was equipped for zoology anyway, and botany always seemed a kind of sissy sort of science - girls only you know. Of course, having now turned into one myself, as it were....'

'No. I just told you that there is nothing of that kind among us. We are all identical - in function. A one sexed race if you like. However it does normally require two such to reproduce. There are examples of such on Earth, even in the animal kingdom - the common or garden snail for instance.'

'Oh.' That was news to me. For an immature alien who had never set foot on the place, J'sati seemed to know an awful lot about the Earth.

'It's all in your memories - unconscious as well as conscious. You must have heard or read it at one time, and forgotten. But it's hardly important. Sufficient that you're aware of the basics. Of course the differentiation amongst plant life-forms has always been more varied - probably to do with their greater versatility and adaptability because they've been around for so much longer.'

'I suppose so.' I felt a strange feeling of inner turmoil welling up inside me - as if I could sense that J'sati was about to launch another mind-bending broadside.

'This is relevant to our present discussion? The reproductive habits of vegetables?'

'Well of course. Why do you think the colour of your skin is green?'

'You mean....' It was surely a joke. 'Not.... not, chlorophyll?'

'Close enough. As I said, we're a very old, very long lived race. What are the longest lived items on Earth?'

'Trees,' I answered stupidly, 'Giant trees.'

'Precisely. Plant life has always been much more adaptable than animal life - probably why intelligent plant life is so rare - no need for it under most circumstances. Clearly once intelligence DID develop, ambulation became a must. And once a plant starts taking on most of the attributes of an animal, then it naturally has to start to resemble it to a certain extent. But of course direct conversion of radiant energy, taking in nutriment directly through the pores of the skin still remains the main source of "food", even though we can actually eat and digest protein, sugars and other energy carrying substances if required. The breeding process....'

'No more just yet awhile, please!' I had some quiet assimilation to do. Not a man any more, not human any more, not even a member of the animal kingdom! I closed my eyes, my mind and let the fragments of my sanity spin round at high speed inside my head. ".... and talk of many things, of shoes and ships and sealing wax, and cabbages and kings. And why the sea is boiling hot, and whether pigs have wings." A cabbage? I had drifted inevitably back to the mirror, hands holding my hair back off my face. More of a giant leek perhaps, crossed with a floribunda rose - did they come with orange blooms? Two things I had always felt could never affect me personally were pregnancy and mildew: how wrong could one be!

J'sati waited patiently in the background. This time I seemed to reach an even keel very much more quickly. I could sense sympathy and reassurance emanating from her - strongly. I was still learning: education through trauma: effective but exhausting. 'All right J'sati. I'm ready for it. The breeding process. Where do the seeds come from, and how do we plant them?'

'Klylii come in only one variety, but two, a full Pair, are required to perpetuate the species. Before that can happen there must be an overwhelming commitment by the Pair concerned. The actual mechanics of the process are, I believe, an extremely moving, prolonged, exhausting and erotic process, and during such activities virtually all external stimuli are cut off or ignored. A time of extreme vulnerability to the Pair concerned. Some two amasts afterwards, one half of the Pair brings forth the single seed,' She held finger and thumb about three inches apart, 'So big, and it is carefully placed in the germinating area where it will grow and develop.' She slipped a finger briefly inside her own belly pouch, 'For a further two amasts. At the end of that time, the seedling - or baby as most prefer to call it, having become too big for the pouch, is removed, and is carried around by and fed as and when necessary by either parent.' She casually flicked a finger against one of her nipples. 'After a further eight amasts the child starts to walk, and is freed of dependence for food on her parents - in theory. In the "wild" the ages from twelve to eighteen (amasts) would have been spent very largely in water, for the complete energy absorption cycle does not become fully operational until then, by which time mentation is properly under way, and the first level is fully open, thus allowing proper two-way communication between the child and her Parent. The next forty amasts are spent growing physically to full size, and the following sixty takes care of most of the necessary mental development - by which time the child looks, and acts, and thinks, pretty well the way I do right now.'

'I see. I get the impression that the pre-requisite, the actual "Pairing" is a pretty special event - where two minds actually merge into a single personality, was the way you described it earlier.'

'Yes. It's a sort of natural progression: falling in love raised to the nth power. The couple involved simply spend more and more time engaged in Communion, which proceeds through deeper and deeper levels as the urge to get closer grows ever more keen. Finally they just.... sort of slip into each other, and the situation becomes permanent - Pairing, or Conjunction. The new Pair then chooses a new personal name for Herself, normally alluding to those of the Single making up the Pair. For example, my Parent chose "Sf" as being made up of parts of "As" and "Ef". When the Singles involved have different family names the "Senior" family name is normally the one selected.'

'Senior?'

'There's a complex hierarchy of family names - I don't fully understand it myself, which basically devolves to an order of precedence allied to the number of members that have been Kaelyj or served as Councillors. I'm not even sure how the listing goes, except that "Laa" is the most senior, and "Ti" stands at number three. Of course in higher level Conjunctions there's a weighting factor covering time, and a relative composition factor that has to be utilised as well.'

'Higher level Conjunctions? You mean that you can get more than two individuals merged into a single ego?'

'Oh yes. Tetrads are not all that uncommon - one forms itself maybe every ten euns or so. And Troikas have been known also. They're very rare though, it being more likely for two Pairs than for three Singles to Unite. I think there has over all our history, been one example of a Grouping of six, but quite a number of eights. None at the present time though of course. The current Kaelyj is a Tetrad - there were no other higher Conjunctions on Klyl when the ship left.'

'Interesting. Presumably such Conjunctions, having twice the brain of a.... Single, or better, tend be much cleverer, more intelligent, get all the top jobs.'

'Well, of course. Everything's a matter of upward progression, improving oneself, that's why nobody under "G" ranking, ever Pairs. It's not forbidden, or impossible, just never seems to happen.'

'Fascinating.' And I meant it, but couldn't help feeling that it was perhaps a trifle advanced for such a very new raw tyro as myself. *'Must take an awfully long time to get round to Pairing then, if one has to work oneself up through the ranks first. "C", "D", and "F" to get through first.'*

'Not as long as all that. Everyone is born and brought up with a grade of "G" or better. If you get Called as a "C" then it's unlikely you'll ever work yourself back up past "D", certainly unlikely to pass "F". There has never, I believe, been a Lyj, who's constituent members were ever Called below "H". But all this is empirical, There's no law or reason, and heroic exceptions exist in every generation. Of course for obvious reasons Pairs always come from Singles of the same grade. It's also rare for Pairing to take place with either being younger than fifty lamasts, but not unknown, especially among close siblings.'

'Siblings! You mean, two children of the same parents, they are allowed to Pair? Is that.... genetically desirable?' The idea was somewhat shocking to a mind that had been imbued from an early age with a horror of incest.

'Oh yes. Very desirable. And a very high proportion of Unions are indeed between siblings. My own parents were born of the same Parent - less than five amasts apart, and Paired when they were less than ten lamasts of age. But then they were ship born and are probably not typical of the race, though VERY typical of this ship.'

'Seems to be quite an unconscious process of natural selection then, if only people of "G" rank and above ever Pair, and hence reproduce.'

'Indeed yes,' J'sati enthused, 'And very right and proper too. Continuous improvement is the name of the game. One must keep ever climbing, or else decline and die. Mind you, it's a very slow process for the lower grades, which make up ninety-nine percent of the race, live just as long.'

'I see.' I wondered how much of the process had derived naturally, and how much had been engineered. A really delightfully simple way of ensuring that only the very, very fittest survived to breed. So unlike the human race that seemed determine to disadvantage any and every sign of success, and encourage the least fit of all to flood the community with congenital misfits of every kind that merely drained the lifeblood of a society that wasn't even allowed to call them the idiots and cripples that they were. 'The.... lower grades, don't feel resentful at all.... No, of course not. It would all come out in the wash - during The Consensus. A place for everyone, and everyone in her place.'

'We like it,' was J'sati's bald comment, 'Could hardly be otherwise, after all, it's being going a long time. And now, my dear H'orlaa,' she continued, 'Enough of the history, biology, philosophy lesson. It's time to get to work.'

'Work? You mean actually DO something.' I was astounded.

171

'Oh no, nothing like that. But YOU, have got much to learn - three new senses to become acquainted with, and one that needs a lot of development. I work hard teaching - you will work even harder learning!'

She had me lie down on the bed - head outwards. *'Now close your eyes - tightly,'* I was commanded, *'And keep them so until I advise you otherwise. Now I'm standing, as you remember, on your right hand side. If your feet are pointing due north, where am I?*

'East south-east.'

'Good. Now I've moved. Where am I now?'

'How can I possibly know the answer to....' I concentrated. *'South.... with a bit of west in it?'* I hazarded, totally at random.

'You can do better than that.' I tried to visualise the room in my mind, imagined the thought stream as a visible link between us *'North west.'*

'That's better. Now where am I?'

'.... west, south-west.'

'Excellent. Now I'm going to speed up.'

For some five asts she flitted around at random, getting faster and faster, and quicker and quicker I had to track her elusive presence, firing back her position. Very quickly I had to switch to a three-hundred and sixty degree notation to keep pace with her movements. Then I lost her.

'Come on H'orlaa, where am I?'

Desperately I searched round, unaware of what I was doing, then, *'Below me.... and two-hundred degrees.'*

'And now?'

'Still below, thirty-five degrees.'

'Good. And now?'

'Above, eighty-six degrees.'

'Perfect. Now then H'orlaa. How far away am I?'

'That's not fair....'

'Come on. I'm requesting nothing that you can't do. Pull back, reach out, and think. Is it one amadn, ten, a hundred, or what. Think, calculate, estimate.'

I thought, calculated and estimated. It was no good. *'I'm not quite sure exactly what a lamadn is,'* I eventually offered. *'Is that something I missed out on?'*

'Oh. Maybe it's something I missed. I seem to recall.... Maybe I didn't. Sorry H'orlaa. Forget it for the moment - yes, you can open them again.' She was beside me once more. *'A lamadn is.... Oh here's another conversion table. Same warning as before.'*

I carefully studied the small card that materialised out of nowhere:
It looked like this:

1 Distance Unit	0.2 Millimetres
1 Madn	3 Centimetres

1 Amadn	4.1 Metres
1 Lamadn	0.6 Kilometres
1 Stal	86 Kilometres
1 Mstal	12,400 Kilometres
1 Lamstal	2 Astronomical Units (250,000,000 kilometres)
1 Amfa	0.5 Light Years

So, an amadn was thirteen feet - the next smallest unit an inch. I did some swift figuring - looked back at the Time card. A duo-decimal base. Interesting - applauded by human mathematicians over the ages as the most logical arithmetical system around. I looked at my hand that held the card, and decided that perhaps it was not so very interesting as all that. If Earth with five digits per arm had settled for a decimal notation, what could be more logical than that The Klylii should go for a twelve. And yet, ten fingers notwithstanding, I seemed to recall that humanity had only reached base ten by accident - early societies had used many others, sixty being a prime contender that even yet, retained a strong grip on time and navigation.

I tossed the two cards away from me. *'All right, J'sati I now know how many amadns there are in an amfa. Do we go back into the range finding business again now?'*

'Yes. But before we do,' She shifted herself to the outer doorway of the room, *'You'll need a calibration run. Note well my position - sixty madns distant.'* She vanished, but continued to converse, *'I'm now five amadns distant - in the same direction of course - reply to me H'orlaa*

'What do you want to know?'

'Nothing, just keep sending and receiving. I'm now twenty amadns further away than previously - all right?'

'Perfect. Should there be any difficulty.'

'No. Now. How far away am I?'

It was examination time once more. I re-ran the three earlier interchanges over to myself, comparing and contrasting. There were overtones that indicated.... *'Ten amadns?'* I suggested hesitantly.

'Not bad, not bad at all, but I think you can do better. Try fining it down a bit.'

'Um.... Eleven amadns less some forty madns.'

'Very good. Now where am I. Distance and direction, three co-ordinates. Horizontal plane as before, vertical at right angles, zero degrees overhead, and all distances in twelfths of an amadn - let's make that brain work a little.'

I struggled, finding it at first easier to lie down on the bed with my eyes closed, but eventually found that I could pinpoint her location precisely with myself in any position and attitude. After spending some twenty asts playing that game, J'sati returned to the room. She sat down on the bed, cross-legged facing me, and bade me adopt the same position.

'Now comes the really easy part H'orlaa. The easy part that is probably the most difficult. Fold your arms, close your eyes, and relax. Now think at me - you can

identify precisely where my head is: one hundred and three madns away from your own, two-hundred sixty-four degrees horizontal, ninety vertical. Yes?'

'Yes.'

'Now try and think ROUND me. I'm stretching both arms out on a level with my shoulders. Try and sense the position of my right finger tip.... now my left. I'm raising my right arm upwards slowly. Track that fingertip! Now where's the left one? My right toe?'

It was hopeless. Time after time I lost track.

'I though you said it was easy?' I complained after nearly ten asts of fruitless contortions by her and wild guesswork on my part.

'It should be. I wonder now. Hmmm, let's see' There was a brief tickling like sensation deep, deep down in my head: it felt as if it were about three feet deep, if my head had been big enough, and then a bright flash of light that had no colour, and at the same time every imaginable colour, exploded outwards from the same inaccessible place.'

'What....'

'Right fingertip moving up.... Stopped now. Position!' She overrode my querulous complaints.

'Fifteen degrees off vertical.... Why, I seem to be able to.... How did that.... You did something to my mind J'sati, don't attempt to deny it!'

'Of course I did, and you should know by now that denial is impossible. Do you mind - track my fingers, my toes - sense my position, all of me, sense it in relation to the bed, the bed in relation to the room. I told you it was easy, you just needed a little push in the right direction, that's all. Now reach out and find the hairbrush. On the table under the mirror. I'm going to move it about. Track it, follow it, sense its position, its orientation - where is it now, which way up? Now? And now? Good. Very good.'

It went on, almost ceaselessly. Lesson after lesson. There were no tea-breaks - Klylii didn't normally drink; no lunch-hours - Klylii very rarely eat; no time off for sleep - Klylii didn't need to sleep very often. I gradually acquired rudimentary knowledge of the universe around me - a knowledge independent of eyes and ears and nose and hands. I learned to inter-relate and integrate all those different Universes: the seen, heard, perceived, smelt and touched worlds about me with an accuracy previously unbelievable. After some five masts of continuous exercises, J'sati called a halt.

'I think you deserve a break. Your brain is as fresh as ever, but that mind of yours still thinks that the odd nap is good for a body - and it is, though not quite so prolonged or often as it imagines, at least, not in an environment where there is ample energy and more, freely available. Let's have a swim, then I'll leave you in peace for a while.'

In the water she ceased to be my serious tutor, and became the child she insisted on declaring herself to be, and after a very short period sitting on the edge, dangling my legs in the water and envying her like hell, I decided that I must really be even more of a child myself, and slipped in to join her cavortions. It was exhilarating - great fun. I hadn't enjoyed myself so much in decades!

But everything has to be paid for. That hour (sorry, those ten asts) spent chasing and being chased, ducking, diving and wrestling, although followed by an unknown period of restful sleep, heralded a stretch of five masts wherein I once more sweated (metaphorically) at the behest of J'sati to acquire the rudiments of yet another skill, to develop one more dormant sense. That poor inoffensive object, the hairbrush, was the victim as I was encouraged to try and move it about. It was a long uphill struggle, even after I had seen and finally understood the first glimmerings of how it all worked, but by the end of the first session I was able to move the brush freely around the room, keeping it aloft for as long as required. And to prove the point was then made to perform similar antics with other objects, both larger and smaller. The next bit was more complex, but only a follow on, and that involved manipulating parts of items - opening the lid of a box, sliding drawers in an out, pulling back bed-coverings and so forth - more fun than work really. Then came the hard part:

'Now concentrate on the table top,' J'sati commanded. 'And externalise the entire concept of the object's "hairbrushness" so that it ceases to be here,' she indicated the brush lying passively on the bed between us, 'And becomes there, over in the middle of the table. Go on, you can do it - try.'

I tried. The brush twitched and vanished, but nothing appeared on the table. 'Sorry. I sort of lost my grip on the destination there.'

'Yes. And I'm afraid it's gone for good. You must be ABSOLUTELY firm, maintain a close grip at all times. Establish the destination co-ordinates with full definity - in fact you must lock them in. There's an area of memory.... Here, let me show you.... No, open up. Let me in.... that's better, just relax. Here, and here, and here. Now set up....' An identical hairbrush to the vanished article appeared on the bed between us. J'sati continued, '.... the destination .... place it there,' I could sense the not unpleasant tingling sensation of J'sati's probing thought-tendrils slipping through and amongst the sections of my mind. 'See, it remains inviolate. Now grasp the brush. Hold it.... Remember there's a brush-shaped quantity of air involved that must be simultaneously moved in the reverse direction. Store that.... good, I see you've anticipated me. Now. Do it!'

And that time the brush did re-appear on the table - with a slight clatter. It had materialised several distance units (dns) above the table top.

'A common error,' J'sati consoled me. 'Everyone does it to begin with, and even skilled operators occasionally don't get it quite right. Experience will teach you to narrow the gap until it's imperceptible, but it's vital that you don't stray in the opposite direction - trying to materialise a brush inside the table would be spectacular, to say the least. Fortunately it's self correcting so that accidental concurrence is impossible, even for beginners, so long as you ensure that there's always a counter-shift. It will rapidly become automatic, because if it doesn't....' There was a loud "bang" from the direction of the table, and the brush reappeared between us.

'That was the air imploding into the space left by the brush. You probably felt the outward surge of the displaced air above the bed as a momentary draft against your thigh.'

I hadn't really noticed it, the "bang" had been a distraction, but thinking back.... I was getting quite expert at replaying events in memory - a very useful feature, especially as it didn't seriously discommode current thinking. Indeed it was a skill that had sort of crept up on me insidiously whilst otherwise engaged, and was only a relatively small part of being able to do or think of several unrelated things simultaneously.

The next step was to change the orientation of the object being "shifted", that is, invert the hairbrush whilst in transit - the trickiest part being the reciprocal movement of the counter-balance. But all that was only a preliminary to the hardest, most complex, most difficult and most dangerous lesson of all: that of shifting myself! That was a whole order of magnitude different from what I'd been doing up until then. Oh, a lot of the peripherals bits were similar - some parts easier: for example it was unnecessary to establish one's own spatial position prior to a shift, for that information was constantly (and automatically) available from a previously unexplored section of brain who's job it was to do just that. And with such exact data always available, it was likewise unnecessary to do more than establish the epicentre of one's destination volume. The really hard part was actually letting go and launching oneself into the gaping void in nothingness that lay between the "here" and "there". It was frightening, the danger of following the first hairbrush into oblivion being a very real, if statistically unlikely, possibility. The odds were actually twenty to one, though J'sati did not tell me that until AFTER I'd made my fourth jump. The odds following a successful first leap, she assured me, rose to some thousands to one against; millions after the second, and ceased to have any meaning following the third.

'So you're perfectly safe now. In point of fact, you were pretty secure anyway. There have been some who've lost up to ten "hairbrushes" in a row. I didn't like to mention it at the time in case you got over-confident, but only one loss is pretty good. I disposed of three! That one in six is simply an overall proportion. Some "trainees" just never seem to reach the stage of gaining confidence, and simply have to make a blind leap with maybe only an even chance of coming out of the other end.'

But I wasn't allowed to rest on my laurels. I was soon hard at it again, learning some of the myriad variations: shifting from a moving position such as running; shifting INTO a moving position; shifting from air into water, or vice-versa (one has to do a three way return shift involving spreading the displaced water over the surface - or collecting it from there) and surprisingly tricky, taking objects with you during a shift. It's amazingly easy to forget to "add" that piece of equipment clutched in one's left hand. Indeed, it's actually easier to "send" inanimate objects fractionally ahead of oneself, picking them up again on the emergence. It would actually be quite complex if one wore a lot of clothes - possibly one of the main reasons why The Klylii used none. One other being of course the need for the external sensors (hair) to be properly free and exposed.

Taking other animate objects along with one during a shift required much more care and it was usually better to actually grip hold of the other person and do a properly integrated scan, temporarily including them as part of one's own intrinsic "aura" that was subject to a constantly automatic update - that meant that any sudden convulsions wouldn't deprive the accompanied one of, say, a wildly failing hand.

It was hard work, but companionable fun, and the more I learnt, the more I discovered about myself, the more it seemed there remained to know, and I was looking forward to an indefinite period spent in the warm companionship of J'sati, getting to know her even better, when suddenly it all ended.

One "morning", after a reasonable sleep, and following an unusually long session, H'fajw, the leader of the Ship Council turned up together with a very despondent J'sati, and austerely advised me that I would have to continue my development on my own for some time to come.

'You have still very much to learn H'orlaa, but although it may be very enjoyable for the two of you, there is not a lot that J'sati can effectively help you with from now on. And in any case, busy times approach, J'sati can no longer be spared to provide individual tuition.'

'I have to continue on self-development here?'

'Continue yes, but not here.'

'Not here?'

'No. Time is running out, in more ways than one. The best place for you to complete your progression is on.... Earth'

'Earth!' It was J'sati who came out with the shocking exclamation, *'But H'orlaa has only just escaped from that horrible place! You surely cannot mean that you want her to return so soon, before she....'*

'J'sati! If you cannot control yourself better than that, I will be forced to forbid you from being a party to these proceedings. Now please, try for a little more decorum.'

'I'm sorry.' J'sati moved closer to me, and slipped her hand in my mine. I could sense her sadness - I could sense my own at the imminence of parting.

'Very well.' H'fajw seemed only partially mollified. *'H'orlaa has much personal development to complete before she can be Called. Much of such work it is considered would be more effectively carried out in a position remote from.... the rest of.... her people. And the human, Mark Richards, left its natal planet with much left undone. That is an omission for which much regret has been felt by all concerned - not least I feel sure by H'orlaa. A spell spent back on Earth will, therefore, provide the opportunity to both tidy up the affairs of Mark Richards, and help H'orlaa's development. A period of no greater than.... two human years should be ample for both.'*

'Two.... eight amasts!' I was horrified, and felt J'sati's distress as keenly as my own.

'Come now - eight amasts is a an extremely short period. It could have been longer, but J'sfti is of the opinion that to leave it any longer would unnecessarily delay the next Ship's Consensus. We shall be within reach of Earth in just over one mast. J'sati, I rely on you to ensure that H'orlaa is fully prepared for transfer by then.' She softened slightly, *'The time will soon pass. You will both be kept busy, I'm sure.'* And on that hopeful note she vanished.

I think that both J'sati and I were somewhat surprised to realise just how much the knowledge of imminent parting was affecting us - for she was reacting as much to my sorrow as I was to hers. It was a somewhat harrowing time of which more might have been made had we not been almost shocked at the sudden revelations that we had been forced to make about ourselves and each other. There was even an element of shamefacedness - I at what might be considered a certain amount of disloyalty to past allegiances, she at her extreme immaturity - and towards the end of the mast allowed, a certain reticence had crept into our relationship.

J'sati took me to the great hanger, where I had arrived centuries ago (about seven weeks) where waited D'nelaa, H'fajw and J'sfti in the person of J'efti. J'sati hung back, suddenly throwing both arms around me, burying her head in my left shoulder. Convulsively I clutched her, digging my own head deep in amongst her tresses. It was a revelation, that brief third level Communion, and taught me more about myself, and J'sati, and being a Klylii than had anything before.

The other three waited patiently and sympathetically aboard the circular landing vessel until eventually J'sati managed to tear herself away. *'Take care....'* was the last vanishing concept left with me as she abruptly shifted the length of the ship away. I moved into the interior of the small saucer shaped craft, and J'efti signalled for D'nelaa to commence the departure sequence.

'Eight amasts is ample time for you to complete both tasks H'orlaa,' H'fajw repeated. *We shall pass back this way again in approximately that time. I would advise you to be ready for departure after six, certainly by the time seven have elapsed.'*

'Oh.' So there was no set time for collection. *'How will I know when the time is come to depart - there are always a few last details that cannot necessarily be left at an instant's notice.'*

'When the time approaches, you will know.' J'sfti stated categorically. *'Of that you will be in no doubt - even before that time you will know that you will know. And now, farewell for a while, H'orlaa.'* She winked out of existence.

The craft had left the ship. In the great curving view-screen (which I had thought windows on my first trip) I could see the retreating bulk of the mother ship and, though of surprisingly little interest, the distant crescent of the Earth, with the much bigger three-quarter illumination of the Moon.

I watched the ship until it was out of sight.

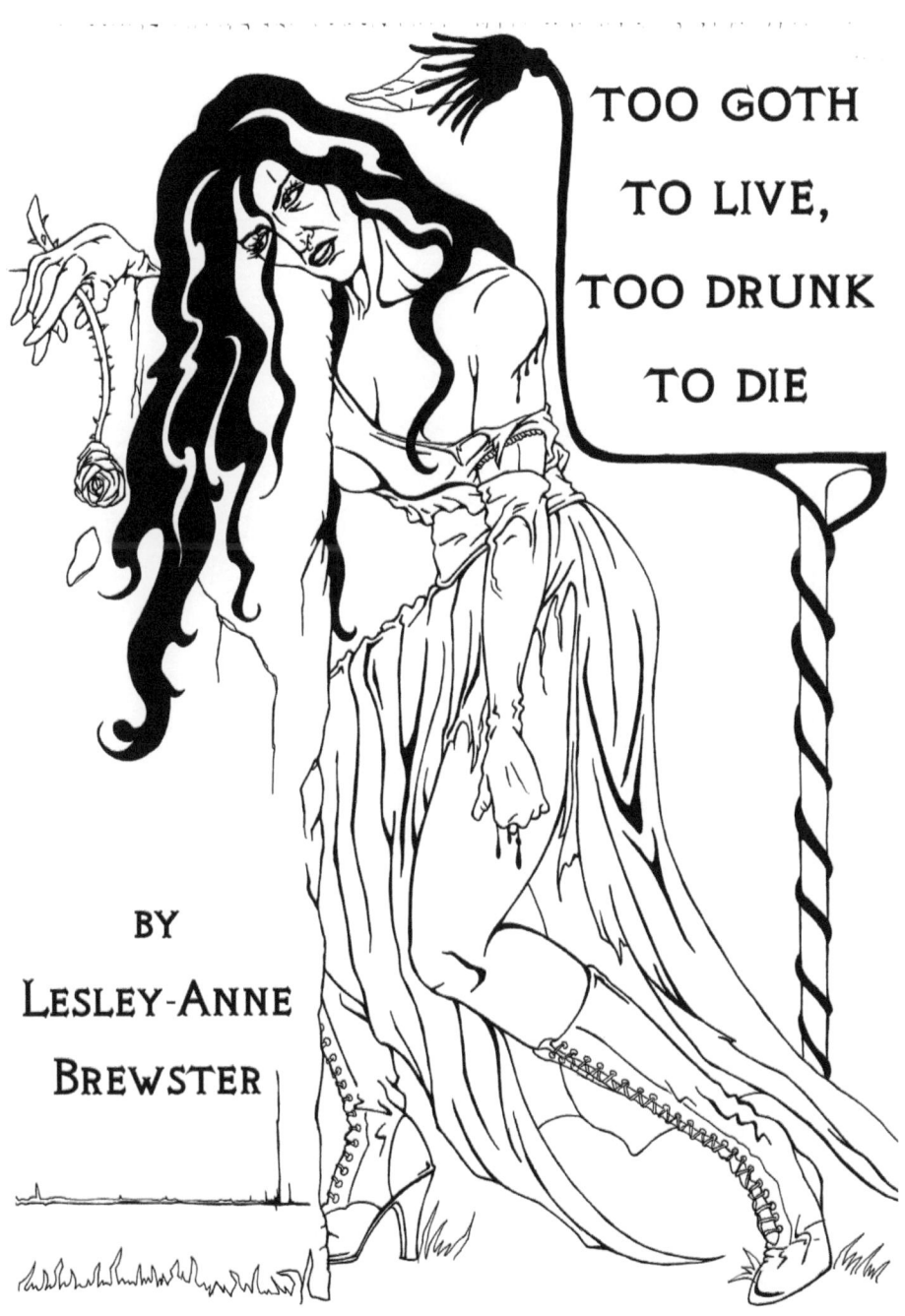

Illustration by Chaz Wood

Love Death – say No to Life. Ha creeping ha.

Life started going downhill when I turned five. I hated school. Still hate school. Hate school. Good name for a movie, that. I hate my parents. Hate. Despise. Detest. Loathe. Both my parents. Daresay a psychiatrist could make money out of that, but…Dad is just a boring know-all, and my mum's a boring nag; a boring nag who doesn't even shave her legs. She hates my friends.
    The irony in that is: so do I. Especially Crystal.
    Crystal knew I fancied Si. I know she knew. I even think I told her. In the shopping centre, just after we'd boosted all that skull stuff out of Claire's accessories. I'm positive I did. We were going on about the things that get you creamy; things, and people; and I'm sure I mentioned Si.
    Si is the baddest side of weird: wild, dark and thin and beautiful. Like, if he was a animal, he'd be a panther. Whereas Crystal; with her cigarettes and glitter wands and stolen laxatives…She'd be a jellyfish; maybe a slug. One of those gross ones: soft and squidgy, trailing snotty slime. It'd be enough to make you puke, except she's cornered that as well.
    She's no more Wiccan than the Duke of sodding Edinburgh. Her mum is just a boring baggy hippy with a black cat that's not even black all over, and a crappy little crap shop full of incense, tinkly music, shiny stones and smeary shelves. If you were psychic, you'd be bound to know your daughter nicked your plop pills.
    And you'd know where Lindl went.

Fuck, I miss Lindl. Hate her, too, for going. If Lindl had've got with Si, that would have been, if not alright, at least okay. Although he would have seen the scars and burns all down her belly and her legs. I did. She might have cut for him. He might have even licked her blood. His sliding tongue behind the razor…
    Only, Lindl disappeared. Her foster family- boring, boring, boring, boring people, live like ads for fabric softener: 'We can't think why she would run away'. Can't think, won't think. They said she didn't even pack a bag. She's likely someone else by now; or lying in a ditch somewhere, as cold and quiet and dead as I would like to be. Still hate her, though.
    If she'd been here, we might have gone together.

What's the point in living ? Hours and days and weeks and months and years and years of work and debt and dust and sitting watching tv, getting gross and sick and slack and old; all helpless against the laughing, meat-breath bullies; against heartbreak, wars and governments and animals being tortured, and the threat of Global Warming. Feeling scared and faking happy till the lights behind your eyes go out. To Hell, I say, with that.

I sold my leather coat to Wolf to buy this booze. He'll likely wear it to my funeral. Then he and Fangs and Si will hit the drink, supposing there's a funeral tea. But Crystal, she'll pig out on all the trays of sweaty sandwiches. Pig slowly, like she does; one little plateful at a time. One tiny mouthful at a time, and always chewing, chewing, chewing, so it all chucks back up as smooth as toothpaste.

I so hate her.

I suppose I should hate Si. I should. I can't. I keep remembering that Friday night, the weekend after Lindl vanished. When I wore the retro ball gown and he quoted Marlowe at me : 'This is Hell; nor am I out of it', and then proceeded to get out of it, on beer and Sebor absinthe. He was on the point of kissing me, I'd swear he was, down in the taxi queue that night. He had my chin cupped in one hand, stroking my hair back with the other. It was raining, tiny rain, and everything was super-bright, and sort of echoing and blurry; everything except his eyes.

Then Crystal noticed he was wearing Lindl's ring, the silver deaths head; made some barf-bitch dig about it, like, had he copped off with Lindl on the sly. So he broke away from me. He wasn't angry. He was flat calm. Just said Lindl'd given him it the night we all went to the cinema, because she had to wash her hands clean of the popcorn grease and didn't want to lose it; and that he'd forgotten to give it back, or she had forgotten to ask him for it. Which was odd, since Lindl always carries hand wipes - but he'd had to tell bulimia incorporated something, I supposed, to shut her up.

Well, then my taxi came; and Wolf says Si got tired of waiting and decided to walk home. And doesn't Crystal live up Si's way? So they ended up together. Even though she knew I fancied him.

My life is over, and it sucked.

I've choked down all the booze I could. But I'm not drunk enough to die of it, I don't think. I'm not nearly drunk enough. Besides, I barfed. Call it a tribute to Crystal. And here's a laugh: the pills I bought – the paracetamols, the aspirin-were in childproof bottles. Ha ha. Even sober, I can never work them open. Tried to bite them. Wound up smashing them against a gravestone. Sure, the bottles opened. Burst, in fact. Scattering suicide smarties off into the dark and the rain.

The ones I found had melted; and I think I ate some graveyard dirt. Maybe the germs in it will kill me; or the chill of the tomb I'm lying on.

How very Goth.

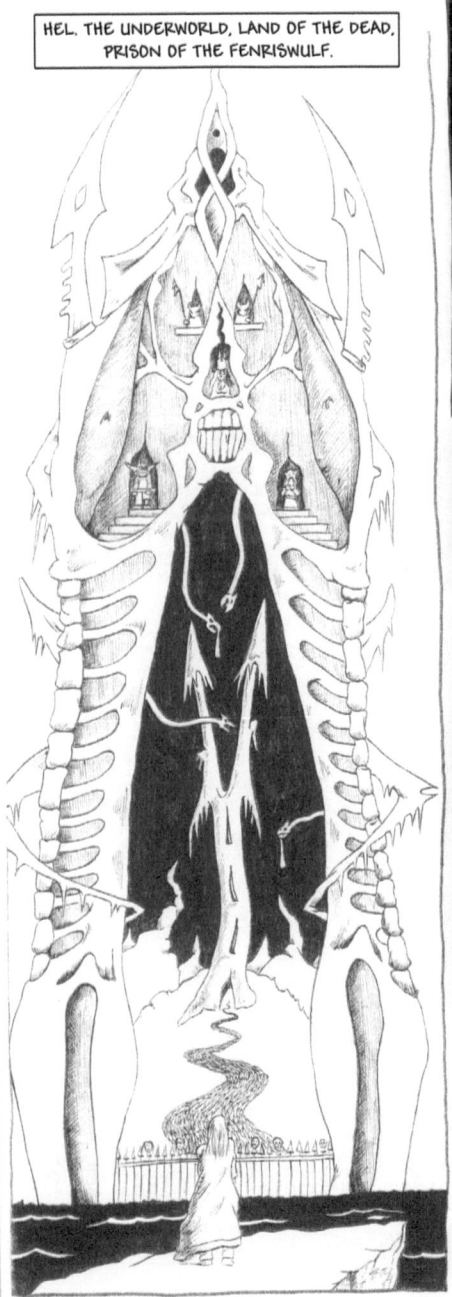

Also Available from Fenriswulf Books

It is the Dawn of the Second Coming
...and the Fourth Reich.

by C. Wood

Available online at amazon, direct from Fenriswulf, and in Dundee's Borders

Dark..chilling..macabre...
A twisted conspiracy of magic, murder,
religion and madness

www.fenriswulf-books.co.uk

www.ingramcontent.com/pod-product-compliance
Ingram Content Group UK Ltd.
Pitfield, Milton Keynes, MK11 3LW, UK
UKHW041438180426
11947UKWH00007B/504